THE FIVE KEYS OF THE SPHINX

By
Joseph Piraino

Published 2006 by arima publishing

www.arimapublishing.com

ISBN 1 84549 157 2
ISBN 978 1 84549 157 4

Printed and bound in the United Kingdom

Typeset in Garamond 11/14

Swirl is an imprint of arima publishing.

arima publishing
ASK House, Northgate Avenue
Bury St Edmunds, Suffolk IP32 6BB
t: (+44) 01284 700321

www.arimapublishing.com

I would like to thank all my friends and family for all their positive support

Best wishes

JPin

Prologue

Have you ever heard of the story concerning the five Sphinxes? May be not. Very few people in existence have ever heard of this tale, because with it, mortal danger will follow. It all started with the goddess Queen Irirus. Irirus was a beautiful woman who looked down on Earth as Earth's guardian. She was so beautiful, that any male creature that gazed upon her would instantly fall in love with her, and do anything for her. For this reason, her extremely strict and formidable father, Poseidon, forbade her from surfacing on Earth. Poseidon was an extremely powerful being, who ruled the oceans single-handed. A large strong man with a very long white beard and a merman's fin, he held a very powerful Trident, which was his sign of the power he possessed.

But Poseidon's warning of not appearing on Earth only fuelled Irirus' longing to go even more. Irirus was fed up with being kept in a prison like state by her father. So, when Poseidon turned away, she crept away and entered Earth. However, on her short time on Earth, she was glimpsed at by a giant red lion beast, that had large skeletal wings and a scorpion's tale. It was a Manticore. (You have got to know that before humans walked the Earth, other strange animals lived on it).

The Manticore loved Irirus the moment he saw her, like any other male creature would. He loved everything from her knee length silver hair and aquamarine eyes, to her perfect hourglass figure and smooth delicate skin. He wanted her desperately. He placed an enchantment on himself to turn himself into an extremely handsome beast, which Irirus fell in love with. They married not long after and she soon fell pregnant. However she gave birth to creatures unlike anything ever seen before. She gave birth to quintuplet females. They had women's faces, yet they were lion bodied and bore scorpion stings as tails. They had soft feathery white wings protruding from their backs. Irirus could not understand why she had given birth to these unknown creatures. The Manticore felt ashamed that he had deceived his beloved Irirus, and he revealed himself as the monster he was. He turned back to his true form and fled from Irirus and his family and never returned. Irirus spent an entire month in shock, unable to talk. She had given up the will to live and died prematurely at the age of 1054 (gods and goddesses live a lot longer than any other mortal).

For the next three hundred years, the quintuplets were raised by their formidable grandfather, Poseidon and he christened the new species Sphinx. He taught them how to defend themselves and the world if times were bad, like he himself had done countless times before. He showed and taught them how to be great rulers and how to do many other things. All this training had a purpose, for the Sphinxes were to replace their mother as the guardians of the planet.

By the time that they finally entered Earth to take up their duty as its guardians, humans had started to inhabit it. Poseidon told them it was time for them to surface on Earth and take up their duty. They were each to guard a different aspect of Earth. One Sphinx went into the desert (soon to become Egypt), another went into the forests, another into the oceans, another into the sky, and the last went to the mountains.

For many years the Sphinxes protected the world well, and Poseidon had forbidden them to be seen with human eyes as humans were simple minded and wouldn't stop until they had hunted them down. But, it didn't last. The Ancient Egyptians had come to live in the deserts. They spotted the Sphinx gliding overhead one day. This wonderful animal entranced them. They did many things for the Sphinx. They held sacrifices to it as if it was another one of their Gods. In the end, the Pharaoh, Khufu ordered a statue to be built of it. The statue was to be built perfect in every way to imitate the Sphinx, apart from the face was meant to be his.

Poseidon was absolutely furious with his with granddaughter. He was already very old, older then the Milky Way in fact. He soon died of shame and disappointment. In his time, Poseidon had many powerful and dangerous possessions that if used or placed in the wrong hands could cause dire consequences. The Sphinxes knew this of course, and they knew that the Trident was the most powerful of them all. So they came to an agreement. They would seal away all of Poseidon's powers into a special place, and only those that could collect all of the five keys would be able to claim Poseidon's power for themselves. However, they felt that now the time was also ripe to seal away all the beasts that had been specially created by the Gods, the modern day mythical animals. It was agreed that each of the Sphinxes would have a key to look after and bury themselves away somewhere so that they would be hard to find or detect. The Desert Sphinx was given the job of ensuring that the mythical animals didn't escape again as she was the one that had been seen and set in motion the events that ultimately caused the death of her grandfather.

To this very day only a few people had heard about this story, and all of them disappeared and were never found or heard of again. The story is non-existent in today's world, as all the ones that knew it, kept it deep inside themselves. But could there be one person that still has this story kept deep within their souls, waiting for the right moment to pass it on…

Chapter 1
A Story from Mythology

Katie-Anne Springwood is a young woman who has very high degrees and experience in mythology and archaeology. Katie-Anne is a very pretty woman. She is quite tall and very slim, with chestnut red hair, which was knotted up into a neat bun. She had bright hazel eyes, which were magnified ever so slightly by her frameless glasses. Her lovely light skin is softer than silk and in still perfect condition. She is never seen without her dark red lipstick, which is painted, delicately onto her luscious lips. She always wanted to be a mythologist as she found mythical animals fascinating. When she was a little girl, her father would often tell her stories of Minotaurs and Banshees and all the various people that had come across them and defeated them. She didn't care what era they came from. Her father often told her stories from Greek mythology, the Ancient Egyptians and many more.

When she grew up, Katie-Anne decided to dedicate her life to studying them. She even believed that at one point such animals might have roamed the earth. She was often teased about this when she was a little girl at school, and even now when she suggested it in her workplace, all her colleagues cant help but laughing at her. But Katie-Anne didn't care. One day she was going to prove to them that mythical animals *did* exist even if they didn't now. She often ran the theory of dinosaurs. Many different species of dinosaur have been dug up but there are still many more which have not yet been found. It's the same with mythical animals. They haven't been found yet. But yet again people just laughed at her and wouldn't take her seriously. She didn't care, because she was determined to prove them wrong one day.

One night some time in the spring, Katie-Anne was working quietly in her office late into the night. She was trying to finish a report on

Chimeras, a lion bodied animal, which bore two heads, one of a lion and one of a goat and had a snake for a tail, which she needed for a meeting in the morning. Everyone else had gone home and the building was quite deserted. Her eyes stung with tiredness as she rubbed them with her aching hand. She decided to get up and visit the toilet and dab a bit of water on them. She got up and walked down the corridor, which was completely unoccupied. Katie-Anne walked back into her office a few minutes later. She immediately saw a black leather suitcase on one of her chairs. She sighed. It belonged to Adam Heart, her colleague. They were the only two who worked in this particular office and they were the best of friends. Katie-Anne decided that she would take it home with her and give it to Adam in the meeting tomorrow morning. She walked slowly to her desk and glanced at the granddaughter clock in the corner. It told her that it was twenty-three minutes to midnight. She rubbed her eyes again and proceeded to her desk. She was just about to sit down when she noticed something strange. There was something on her desk, that wasn't there before. Katie-Anne looked at it. It was a yellow folder with the word 'IMPORTANT' stamped across it in red capital letters. Katie-Anne stared at it curiously. *Who on earth could have put this on my desk?* She thought curiously. There was no one left in the office or in the building for that matter, so who or what had sneaked in into her office and placed this folder onto her desk? She wondered if her secretary might have popped it in, as she sometimes stayed quite late. But Katie-Anne remembered that her secretary had been off ill for the past two days. Katie-Anne reached for the package nervously. She picked it up: it was quite heavy. She opened it and a large scroll of blue paper fell out and flumped on to the carpet. As she picked it up, her eyes widened and her eyebrows almost disappeared into her hair, for what was on the paper startled her.

Chapter 2
The Writing on the Tablets

The paper bore pictures of the statue of the Sphinx in Egypt and also pictures of many weird tablets all broken, old and covered in hieroglyphics. One tablet caught her eye. It was in perfect condition and looked as if it had been laminated. It was stuck to a wall in a place that was unfamiliar to Katie-Anne.

Being an archaeologist, Katie-Anne could just translate some of the hieroglyphics on this tablet. However, she opened one of the drawers in her desk and took out a small Egyptian Bilingual dictionary and began translating. The more she translated, the more puzzled and intrigued she became. Eventually, after about thirty minutes work, she managed to have translated it fully. This is what she read:

We saw it, with our own eyes!
The Gods answered our prayers.
They sent a creature to guard us!
We built a statue in its honour with
The face of our dear lord Khufu! We
Tried to appease the beast with sacrifices
But it never returned.

Under the hieroglyphics there was a picture of the Sphinx drawn by Egyptians. Katie-Anne turned the paper over and found a small sentence written in a very untidy scribble

Sphinxes are the riddle masters

This didn't make any sense at all. The tablets said that the Egyptians saw a real live Sphinx yet it is only a statue. Also, someone had written that the Sphinxes are 'Riddle Masters' what ever that's supposed to mean. Katie-Anne was puzzled, puzzled because someone had written the sentence about Sphinx in the plural, even though there is only one, and had said that they are riddle masters. But the Sphinx is not a living creature, and how can it be a riddle master, it doesn't even talk!? *Only in mythology* thought Katie-Anne

What could all this mean? Was this someone's idea for a joke? Had someone gone a step further to punish Katie-Anne for all the rubbish she came out with about mythical creatures once being real? Yet some of the tablets meanings are similar to historical resources. History tells us that an unknown pharaoh to show his sign of power and courage built the statue of the Sphinx. This tablet plainly told Katie-Anne that it was the pharaoh Khufu that had built it, and strangely enough, he was definitely the pharaoh people thought to have built the statue.

Katie-Anne was really tired by now. She decided to fold the paper up and stick it in her handbag and take it to the meeting with her tomorrow. She walked out of her office and locked the door. She continued down the empty corridor, apart from it was no longer empty. There was someone down the corridor, wearing a white uniform, and holding an old mop and cleaning the floor. Katie-Anne was relieved. It was only the cleaner. She knew the cleaner quite well, as she saw her nearly every night. Katie-Anne walked up to the cleaner and she turned around. But there was something wrong, this wasn't the cleaner Katie-Anne knew. This cleaner was a young male, who was fairly tanned and had long dreadlocks. A small goatee was beginning to grow on his small chin.

"Oh! Sorry, I thought you were someone else," said Katie-Anne apologetically. "Do you know where Fiona has gone?" Fiona was the cleaner she knew very well.

"Fiona got a new job somewhere in Coventry. I'm her replacement, Solomon," replied the stranger.

"Oh, nice to meet you, I'm Katie-Anne Springwood," and they shook hands. She began to walk away, when she turned back round.

"Solomon? Did you by any chance see anyone down here in the last ten minutes or so?" asked Katie-Anne hopefully.

"Apart from you, no miss," and he retuned to mopping the floor. Katie-Anne turned away and continued walking. She took the lift down and she walked into the car park and unlocked her car.

All the time while she was driving, she just kept thinking about what she had discovered in her office. She didn't even remember unlocking her door and going inside her house, but she must have done because next second she was putting on her pyjamas and taking off her glasses as she climbed into bed. She turned the lights off and fell asleep

Katie-Anne could hear something in the distance. She woke up with a start to find her mobile phone ringing. She answered it. It was Adam.

"Kate, where are you? The meeting started a half hour ago! We need you here, now!" Katie-Anne swore loudly and hung up the phone. She quickly got dressed and took a packet of bread and a tub of butter with her into the car to eat while she drove.

Katie-Anne drove well over the speed limit and quite badly as she was rushing to get to work and eat her breakfast at the same time. She couldn't work out why she had slept so long, it wasn't like her at all to be late for work, and especially not when she had a big meeting to attend.

At last Katie-Anne reached her workplace. She flew by her doorman and up the lift. She hammered the buttons hard.

"Come *on!*" she roared angrily at the lift. At long last, she arrived at the right floor. She stopped abruptly at the door and knocked quietly and entered. The room was very big. A table was in the centre of the room and it stretched the width of the room. There was no back wall; it was just one enormous window. About fifteen men and about six women were sitting around the large varnished table.

"Ah, I'm glad you could join us Miss Springwood," spoke an elderly man at the head of the table. This was Winston Firebell, Katie-Anne's boss.

"Sorry I'm late Mr. Firebell, I had a really late night last night," replied Katie-Anne quietly. She quickly closed the door and took a seat at the only remaining chair. Her colleague, Adam Heart was sitting opposite her. His small grey eyes were looking anywhere but at Katie-Anne. His short gelled black hair ruffled slightly in the air conditioning.

"Now we are all assembled we can now continue," Mr. Firebell began. "I believe we were discussing the case of new evidence that there may be tombs buried within the statue of the Sphinx in Egypt. Of course, this could be a hoax, as we have had so many before. But I believe this time it may be right. I think we should make a formal investigation of this before another company does. We need a bit of glory for a change." Silence greeted these words. "Now Clancy"- he addressed a woman who was sitting on his left hand side-"I believe you have your hands full at the moment with the discovery of a pterodactyl fossil which may well be a new species." The woman called Clancy nodded. Winston Firebell now addressed a man sitting next to her, "Michael, I believe you are making an investigation on the discovery of the bones of a new sea creature found on the borders of Cornwall. You obviously can not do this either." At this point Katie-Anne began to speak.

"I'll be able to do it," she said enthusiastically.

"You, Miss Springwood?" said Mr. Firebell curiously gazing at Katie-Anne as if he had never seen her before. Every eye in the room was upon Katie-Anne. "I thought you were beginning to make a detailed investigation on the sighting of a Chimera?" Nearly everyone in the room snorted and sniggered. "And do you have that report for us?"

"I do sir. I want to investigate the Sphinx because I have a reason to investigate it anyway," she said, ignoring all the sniggers that were echoing around the room.

"And why do you need it investigate the Sphinx, Katie-Anne?" Firebell asked suspiciously. Katie-Anne unclipped her handbag and took out the heavy blue paper that she found on her desk the previous night.

"I have here," she began, "evidence that the Sphinx is a real animal!" This time there was no light sniggering but a roar of laughter. Everyone

14

in the room, apart from Adam and Firebell were laughing at Katie-Anne. Yet again Katie-Anne was unperturbed by it. *I will show them!* She thought savagely, *stupid people! They will regret this when I prove to the world that I was right all along!*

"I have here!" she shouted over the noise from the laughter, "evidence that the Sphinx exists! Last night, when I was working in my office, I slipped out to get some water, and when I returned, this was laying on top of my desk." She slid the blue paper against the vanished top of the table to Firebell. He caught it and began to look at it.

"But obviously this is some kind of joke," laughed Firebell, sharing the joke with all the others.

"I have here," and yet again Katie-Anne unclipped her handbag, "the translation of that tablet." She pulled out the rough piece of paper she used to scribble the translation on. "There is nothing false about that tablet!" said Katie-Anne. Firebell began to hand around the blue paper when Katie-Anne picked up a paperweight from the edge of the table, placed it on top of the translation and slid it to Firebell. He read it aloud to everyone:

We saw it, with our own eyes!
The Gods answered our prayers.
They sent a creature to guard us!
We built a statue in its honour with
The face of our dear lord Khufu! We
Tried to appease the beast with sacrifices
But it never returned

"Do you know who sent you this?" Firebell asked on a more serious note. No one was laughing any more, and on the contrary they all looked genuinely curious.

"No. It happened late last night. Like I said, I went to get some water and when I came back this was on my desk inside a folder." The people around the table began whispering to each other. Firebell was eying the blue paper suspiciously.

"But obviously anyone could have put this on your desk as a joke?" said Firebell.

"I don't think so somehow. The building was quite deserted when it happened apart from the cleaner I saw. But I hardly feel a cleaner would want to do something like this." Firebell placed his fingers together and contemplated what Katie-Anne had just said. He sat silently for several seconds, and then he broke out of his reverie.

"Ok, I will fund your trip to Egypt to let you explore the Sphinx. You may investigate this thing, this fantasy about living Sphinx but I would like your main priority to look for the tombs, understand?" asked Firebell.

"Yes, I understand sir," replied Katie-Anne gratefully.

"I suppose Mr. Heart will be joining you?" asked Firebell. He looked at Adam. To Katie-Anne's amazement he nodded.

"Fine. Miss Springwood. May I warn you not to mess this up? This trip will cost the company a lot of money and if you mess it up, you will be out of here faster than you can say 'Sphinx', understood?"

"I do sir," replied Katie-Anne.

"How many men will you require?" Firebell asked, not even looking at Katie-Anne, but shuffling his papers. By men, Firebell meant diggers and archaeologists to help with the digging and exploring. Katie-Anne thought about it for a moment.

"I think we should have twenty at least," replied Katie-Anne at last.

"Consider it done."

*

The rest of the meeting passed slowly. Katie-Anne gave her report on Chimeras and was widely laughed at. But finally they were dismissed and everyone rose from their chairs talking. Katie-Anne was just about to walk out of the door when Adam caught her up.

"Bit suspicious don't you think? You were the only one here last night, how could that folder have ended up on your desk?" he asked suspiciously.

"Well I wasn't the only one here, was I? The cleaner was here as well," Katie-Anne replied.

"You cant- you don't seriously think the cleaner"-

"Of course I don't! But we can't eliminate the fact that he was the only other living soul anywhere near me at the time of the incident." They walked on in silence for a while.

"On the back of the paper, it said something about Sphinx being riddle masters? What is that all about?" asked Adam curiously.

"I have a theory. In fiction, mostly in books, when there is a Sphinx they always talk in riddles, don't they?"

"If you say so," said Adam putting on a puzzled face which plainly said he hadn't read a book of any kind.

"So I'm thinking that whoever gave this to me is trying to tell me the Sphinxes are riddle makers, or masters"-

"So you don't think that all of this is just fiction, depicting what other people have written and thought of?" he asked anxiously. Katie-Anne gave Adam a look as if he had just said something hurtful or deeply offending.

"There is nothing fictional about that tablet!" she said coldly, not looking at Adam. "I know the Egyptians saw something and my job is to investigate it. I thought you would be one of the very few people to believe me, but I see I was sadly mistaken." Adam looked ashamed of himself.

"It's not that I don't believe you," he began after a few seconds silence, "It's just that it seems a little farfetched."

"So, will you help me find out one way or the other?" Katie-Anne asked.

"I think you already know the answer to that." Katie-Anne smiled at him, "When have you ever known me to work against you?"

"Never," replied Katie-Anne. "Oh by the way, I have your black suitcase in my car; you left it in the office last night."

"Thanks," replied Adam. "When do you plan us going to Egypt anyway?"

"As soon as possible. The sooner the better. The quicker we get there the quicker we can get to the bottom of this mystery."

Chapter 3
The Mystery Man

Many months had now passed since Katie-Anne had discovered the folder on her desk. However, these precious months were not wasted as they were spent devising the trip to Egypt, which Katie-Anne had discussed the many months ago. Katie-Anne had a hard time organising with the diggers and archaeologists that Firebell had employed for her, as they kept disagreeing with everything she said. However, she reminded them that she was in charge and if they wanted paying they had better do as she said. This made them fall quiet.

*

Finally the day before the journey to Egypt was coming to a close, and Katie-Anne was doing her last minute packing adding bits and bobs she needed. The weather outside changed rapidly. One moment a shrill cloudy sky, and next an all out thunderstorm, with rain that lashed hard at the windows. It was very dark outside by now. Katie-Anne was just zipping her case shut when her house phone rung. She thought it was probably Adam asking for last minute advice on what to pack. But she was wrong. She picked up the phone. Before she even had the chance to utter a single word, a cold ruff growling voice spoke down the phone.

"You would do well to abandon your project!" it said.

"Hello, who is this?" asked Katie-Anne, a note of terror in her voice.

"You don't know what you're getting yourself into!" it said again, in its unchanging cool sharp growl.

"Who are you? Hello?" but at that moment the cold voice rung off leaving Katie-Anne standing there, transfixed with fright. She threw the phone back onto the hook as if it contained some terrible poisonous disease and she immediately ran to all the doors and windows in the house and locked them. She had become so paranoid that she even forced the poor downstairs bathroom window closed by tying the window handle to the handle of the shower doors with a bit of rope so that no one would be able to open it.

After she had barricaded every entry point in the house, she ran back to the phone and called Adam.

"Hello?" said Adam sleepily on the other end of the phone. Katie-Anne burst into tears.

"Adam, please help me!" she sobbed hysterically, looking around the house as if it frightened her.

"What's wrong, what's happened?" he asked. Katie-Anne told Adam about the man's voice on the phone, crying all the way through, and not even drawing breath.

"Ok, just calm down. Have you locked all your windows and doors?" he asked her

"Yes," she replied.

"Have you called the police?" he asked.

"No, I don't want them to get involved," she said, no longer sobbing.

"Don't you think you should?"

"What can they do about a phone call?. Nothing really, it would just waste their time," she replied

"Ok. Now whatever you do, do not answer the door tonight or the phone. Just let the phone ring and the doorbell, ok?"

"Yes," she said, now calming down totally.

"Put the answer machine on, so if I need to ring you, I can leave you a message to tell you it's me."

"Ok."

"Right. See you in the morning." They said their goodbyes and hung up.

*

The next morning, Katie-Anne woke up early and got dressed ready for the trip. The bus would be leaving in about twenty minutes, so she didn't waste time. She packed her three suitcases into the boot of her car and she drove to her office. There was a white bus parked outside and the driver was fitting the luggage into the compartment at the side. Adam was waiting for her near the bus and he greeted her as she opened the door. Katie-Anne immediately flung herself upon him and did her very best to stop herself from crying.

"Hey, it's alright! He can't get you now, you're safe," he said reassuringly.

"I was so scared!" she murmured into his shoulder.

"It's all over now."

Adam helped her cart her luggage over to the bus and the driver hoisted them into the bus with the others.

"Can you please get on the bus now? We will be leaving as soon as I've finished with this," said the driver. So Katie-Anne and Adam walked onto the bus and saw about twenty people already assembled there. She called for silence and checked them all off on a sheet to make sure they were all there. They were. Katie-Anne took her seat with Adam right at the front of the bus, and Katie-Anne whipped out her laptop and turned it on. The driver entered the bus and turned on the engine. The bus began to move. They were on their way to the airport.

All the way through the bus journey, Katie-Anne studied hieroglyphics on her laptop, and the history of the Sphinx. None of what she was looking at made sense. The statue of the Sphinx was built by command by an unknown pharaoh as a sign of his courage and power. However no one knows which pharaoh built it. However, the tablets suggested it was Khufu. The pharaoh wished it to have the body of a lion to show his courage with his face crafted onto it. Katie-Anne was just taking a closer look when she spotted something that she didn't see before. The statue of the Sphinx had a lion's tail curled round to its hind legs. However, according to the picture she had seen on the blue scroll, the Sphinx had an elongated curved scorpion tail including sting, quivering over the Sphinx's back.

"Adam, look at this!" said Katie-Anne excitedly, tapping his shoulder and showing him the screen.

"Look. The tail of the statue has a normal lion's tail, while the Sphinx picture on the blue paper shows it with a scorpion's tail." Adam grinned broadly at this.

"You see Katie-Anne! Proof! Proof that this whole thing is a hoax. This is nothing but fiction, and this shows it! Not even you can deny it this time!!!" Katie-Anne looked at him with an almost burning stare, and he cowered under her gaze.

"No, I have a different theory!" she said, keeping her voice calm. "History tells us that the Sphinx's behind was much longer. However, it had too much pressure and it collapsed. The Egyptians rebuilt it. I believe that they built the tail of the scorpion first time round, but it was that that had made the behind so unstable. So when they rebuilt it, they left the tail out and put in an ordinary lion's tail instead." Katie-Anne smiled triumphantly. Adam stared pompously at her.

"There is no proof of that!" Adam glowered turning bright red out of either irritation or embarrassment; it was hard to tell. "I still think that we are wasting our time and we will recover nothing out of it. Nothing!"

*

About an hour later, the bus came to a halt. They had stopped so that they could all freshen up and go to the toilet. Most of the archaeologists went to the bar to get drinks and food. Adam and the bus driver went to the gas station to get directions and Katie-Anne went to the toilet. She walked slowly back to the bus, enjoying the fresh air. The bus was only round the corner; there was no need to rush. She just turned round the corner when she caught sight of it. She gave a large gasp in fright and dropped her handbag. She took a few steps closer towards the bus. There were red words spray painted all over the side of the bus, windows and all. They read- "If you do not stop now, you will be in grave peril!" She quickly picked up her handbag and ran as fast as her high heels would take her to the gas station. She forced aside the pneumatic doors before they had even opened properly and saw Adam and the bus driver talking to a tanned man with a small goatee and spiked dark hair. She could have sworn she had seen him somewhere before, but she couldn't think about that now.

"You need to go back to the bus, and see it, now!" she gasped hysterically.

"Why?" asked Adam, looking at her absurdly.

"Someone- words. All over the bus, in red!" she replied. The driver rushed out immediately. Adam and Katie-Anne followed pursuit. They found the bus driver just gaping at the bus. Adam looked at it with a mixture of shock and disgust.

"Adam, can you go round and bring back all the passengers?" Katie-Anne asked. Adam nodded and hurried off. Katie-Anne went over to the bus driver. He was too appalled to speak. Minutes later, Adam returned with all the diggers and archaeologists looking confused. When they all saw the bus there were many different reactions. Katie-Anne turned to face them. Anger was on her face like she had never had before. The passengers actually stepped back from her.

"Does anyone here know who's done this!!?" she shouted angrily using a large number of decibels and pointing to the bus. No one answered her. She took their silence as a no. She knew that none of them knew, but she didn't care.

"None of us 'av been near the bus since we got off," said one of the passengers timidly.

"I want to see all of your hands! If I find a speck of red paint on any of them, I can not possibly describe the trouble you will be in; not only with me, but with the bus company and Mr. Firebell!" No one spoke. They all showed her their hands but they were all clean as a whistle. She ordered them to get back on the bus saying the break was over.

"Should we call the police?" Katie-Anne asked the driver quietly. The driver looked at her.

"No, there's no need to get the old bill involved. No one was 'urt. I scrub this off, don't you worry!" he replied. With that, they entered the bus and they were on their way again. Katie-Anne sat back at the front with Adam.

"Someone obviously doesn't want us on this project," Katie-Anne whispered in his ear so no one else could hear.

"Don't worry. We will be all right once we enter Egypt. The person can't follow us there, can he?"

How very wrong Adam was.

They eventually got to the airport and they flew smoothly to Egypt. It was a very long journey, but Katie-Anne kept with her laptop trying to discover more on this mystery.

After the long flight, they landed in Cairo and they were all taken by another bus to their Hotel. Katie-Anne just stayed in her room and began working on her laptop again. She could hear Adam clanging around noisily next door. While she was working on her laptop, she logged onto the Internet. She found fantasy pictures of the Sphinx with lion bodies but with women's faces and large white feathery wings. This didn't add up. The Sphinx was a hybrid and a very unusual one at that. She sighed deeply and thought. What if Adam was right all along? What if all this stuff about the Sphinx was just one big hoax, and in her desperation to find a living mythical animal she had fallen for it? She hoped not for many reasons, one being that her job could be at stake. At that moment there was a knock at the door. She placed her laptop onto her bed and put her ear against the door.

"Who is it?" she asked.

"It's Adam!" Katie-Anne unlocked the door and opened it.

"Phone call for you in the lobby. I think its Firebell." Katie-Anne walked out with Adam and locked her door. When she got downstairs, an Egyptian manager who spoke English passed her the phone.

"Hello?" said Katie-Anne

"Ah, Katie-Anne. So you got there ok I take it?" came the relieved voice of Winston Firebell. Katie-Anne was on the phone to him for about ten minutes, explaining everything that had happened including the red paint on the bus. Firebell told Katie-Anne that the bus driver had already informed him and luckily was not pressing charges.

Katie-Anne returned to her room after she had finished her conversation. She unlocked the door and screamed loudly. Adam came crashing out of his room and rushed towards her.

"What is it, what's happened?" he asked her. It was quite clear what Katie-Anne had screamed about. All the walls were full of red writing which all bore the same message "YOU HAVE BEEN WARNED!" Katie-Anne immediately rushed down to the lobby to inform the manager who phoned the Egyptian police. The police came shortly afterwards. While they investigated her room, Katie-Anne took Adam aside.

"So, they wouldn't follow us to Egypt would they?" she whispered angrily.

"But I don't understand why someone is going through all the trouble to do this," replied Adam, staring around the room.

"Someone really doesn't want me here!" said Katie-Anne. "I want to know how they got into my room when the door was locked."

"Your right!" said Adam looking fearful, "only a member of staff of the hotel could have gotten in." They both looked around the room. "So, what are we going to do?"

"I tell you what we are going to do. We are going to continue as planned. It will take a lot more than a late night phone call and some red writing to scare me off!" she said confidently. Katie-Anne looked at her bed. It looked oddly ruffled as if something had once been there, but wasn't anymore.

"And this writing isn't all that's been done in this room. The Mystery Man is a thief. My laptop is gone!"

Chapter 4
Monsters Unleashed

"Gone? Are you sure?"-

"Yes, I left it on the bed when I went to answer the phone. I had valuable information on that needed for the project," replied Katie-Anne, brushing her hair backwards.

"Can we still continue?" asked Adam anxiously.

"We can, but we might not be able to excel as quickly as if I had the laptop," replied Katie-Anne. "We leave at dawn."

*

Katie-Anne set her alarm to wake her up very early next morning. She quickly got dressed in her old clothes ready for the investigation on the Sphinx. She woke up Adam and all the archaeologists. After a quick breakfast, they went outside and they all climbed into the Land Rovers they had rented.

They drove for hours before they finally reached the Sphinx. It looked exactly how Katie-Anne imagined it. The Sphinx's face was all cracked and had vastly crumbled away making it illegible. The body of the Sphinx was mostly eroded and its hind legs were barley visible.

The group of people all climbed out of their vehicles and hung about talking in groups. Adam and Katie-Anne walked under the head of the Sphinx.

"So we're here. Now what?" Adam asked impatiently. Katie-Anne turned around.

"Gather round, please!" she yelled loudly so that everyone could hear her. All the archaeologists stopped talking immediately and went and gathered around Katie-Anne and Adam.

"What we are looking for is some sort of entrance into the statue. We need to be careful not to damage the statue, but all the same the entrance must be well hidden so keep your eyes peeled. So split up and if you find anything report to me or Mr. Heart, ok?" she instructed. There was a murmur of agreement and understanding from the group and they all split up with their apparatus and began investigating. Katie-Anne faced Adam again.

"It's a shame the face is eroded," said Katie-Anne disappointedly. "The face would have been the biggest clue we would have needed in solving this mystery."

"Don't you think we should have started by looking for that tablet on the paper you were given?" Adam asked.

"I have a sneaky suspicion that the tablet may be within the Sphinx. And since this whole project is based around the Sphinx, I cleverly came to the conclusion of investigating the Sphinx first," said Katie-Anne sarcastically.

"Ha, ha, very funny. But we still don't know that there is a secret passage into the Sphinx. This statue has been under investigation for hundreds of years and no one has found any such thing! And I thought of another thing. You think that the tablet is inside the Sphinx, yet how would anyone have got a picture of it if the entrance hasn't been discovered?" Adam smiled triumphantly.

"How do we know it hasn't been uncovered? Someone could have uncovered it years ago." Even as she said this Katie-Anne felt her confidence falling. May be Adam was right. This project was probably a clever hoax. Her stomach churned at the very thought. If this was one big hoax then she had cost the company thousands of pounds for nothing. She would be fired…

"I've found something!" shouted one of the many archaeologists excitedly, running forwards towards Katie-Anne. "Look here!" he shouted and pointed right underneath the Sphinx's head. She ran over to it. All the blocks that had assembled the neck area had worn away and they looked as if they had moulded into one. However, there was one block that was more visible than the others, and what was so distinguishable about this block is it had a very strange and intriguing symbol crafted onto it. Katie-Anne wasn't sure what the symbol was. It definitely wasn't any hieroglyphic that she recognised. The symbol appeared to be the shape of dual wings with a picture of the sun in between them.

Katie-Anne slid a finger down the block and over the symbol. Nothing happened. She consulted her hieroglyphics book just to make sure there wasn't a symbol in there that matched the one on the block. As she predicted there wasn't. So what on earth was she going to do now?

"What should we do?" said one of four archaeologists that had crept over Katie-Anne's shoulder for a closer look. Katie-Anne thought about it for a moment.

"Try prising it open with crowbars," she replied. Katie-Anne moved back and watched as the four archaeologists moved forwards wearily, each brandishing a crowbar. The archaeologists jammed their bars randomly around the block and began to push and dig. All at once, the block shined a mysterious blue before turning a murderous red. The block let off an explosive force, which sent the archaeologists flying thirty-two feet backwards, where they landed in a hump on the soft sand. The crowbars were nothing more than melted blue blobs of metal on the sand. The block stopped glowing abruptly.

"What was that about?" Adam asked nervously, looking at the block as if it was about to pass on some infectious disease.

"I don't know," replied Katie-Anne, looking at the block with a bit more thought. She moved towards the block, keeping her eyes on it all the time, just in case it decided to let out another blast.

"Kate!! What are you doing!? Don't go near it; you'll hurt yourself!" Adam shouted sceptically. Katie-Anne chose to ignore him, and carried on forwards to the block. When she reached it, she began dusting it and examining it very carefully. She tried saying things to it in ancient Egyptian, but with no luck. She stared at it hard.

"Of course!" she whispered excitedly. "Quick, someone, give me a magnifying glass!" The archaeologists quarrelled over the tool kit, and one of them returned with a magnifying glass. Katie-Anne took the magnifying glass off the man and tried to angle it so the sunlight reflected onto the block. Unlucky for them, the sunlight was not in the right position.

"Plan B. Who has a torch?" she called. Another archaeologist came forwards this time with a torch. Katie-Anne shone the torch into the magnifying glass and onto the block. All at once, the strange symbol glowed blue and was replaced by hieroglyphic inscriptions. Katie-Anne read them out aloud:

"Only when true light passes over this stone, will those who seek what lurks inside; be aloud to pass."

"And that means...?" asked Adam, peering over Katie-Anne's shoulder.

"It means that we need proper sunlight to pass through the glass and onto the rock in order for it to open. Artificial light, AKA electrical light, doesn't work," she replied. She took the torch and magnifying glass away, and as she did so, the words were replaced with the old dual wings and sun symbol.

"Do we have any mirrors?" she asked the archaeologists behind.

"We have four!" replied one of them nearest the vehicles. He went inside and brought them out. They were only roughly the size of an average stone slab.

"Will they be big enough?" Adam asked anxiously as he watched the four mirrors being brought forward.

"They are perfect," replied Katie-Anne, a huge triumphant grin spreading across her face.

Carefully, Katie-Anne set up the mirrors so that one mirror reflected the sunlight into another, which reflected the light into another, which reflected the sunlight into a third mirror, which reflected the light just above the block in which they were aiming.

"Should I adjust the mirror?" Adam asked.

"No, we will reflect the light through the magnifying glass." She rushed towards the block with the glass in her hand. She angled it carefully and the light shone through onto the block. The symbol on the block shone yellow and the block itself glowed orange. The block retreated into the Sphinx and out of sight. The two layers of blocks underneath also disappeared, leaving a big enough gap for a human to fit through.

Katie-Anne turned round to face her crew, happiness shining all over her face. The archaeologists and Adam were staring at the space in the Sphinx as still as statues, looking unbelievably at it.

"How, how did you know it was going to do that?" Adam asked at last, his voice faint and shaky.

"I really can not be bothered to explain, and I'm pretty sure you lot won't understand it anyway, so I'm not going to bother." She glanced at the opening in the Sphinx, and back again towards her crew. "So, who wants to go first?" They all backed away, murmuring feeble excuses and alibis. "Oh you babies. Fine! I will go first. And if you so called 'MEN' are brave enough to follow me, then you are most certainly welcome to." She put her feet into the gap and slid her body underneath and disappeared.

"She's right you know," said Adam shamefully.

"About being babies?" replied an archaeologist.

"About everything! Wait up Kate, I'm coming too!" Adam walked to the hole and disappeared into also. The archaeologists began shouting their triumph and manliness and one by one they all entered into the hole.

*

Meanwhile, down in the hole, Katie-Anne had switched on her torch. The room inside was as narrow as it was possible to see, and it carried onto a narrow corridor. The walls on either side of them were filled with inscriptions and cobwebs. They began to walk on down the narrow corridor, which didn't go straight ahead, but seemed to be going deeper and deeper, with lots of stairs. As they got further in, small indentations appeared in the walls. Tombs and skeletons filled the indents. They had entered upon an underground catacomb.

"Are these – bodies?" Adam asked fearfully.

"Yes," replied Katie-Anne and she looked at some hieroglyphics that were positioned just above each tomb. "And according to these hieroglyphics-" she moved her finger along the wall "-these people were offered as sacrifices to the Sphinx, just as the tablet depicted!" Katie-Anne swelled with excitement. She continued down the passageway.

It slowly got deeper and deeper. The deeper they got, the more bodies started to appear. They all eventually came to a sudden halt. They had reached a dead end stonewall. Katie-Anne shone her torch on the wall and stared at it. It was completely blank; just an ordinary wall. The happy bubble which had swelled inside her chest at the very thought of finally uncovering the mystery of the Sphinx deflated faster than a popped balloon. She stood there glumly looking at the wall disbelievingly.

"Well, I guess that's all. We should get going now," Adam said quietly behind her. Katie-Anne refused to move. This couldn't be all of it, it just couldn't, and maybe they just missed something, she thought to herself. She finally moved, but not away from the wall, but closer. She reached out her arm and touched the wall, as if she expected it to dramatically respond in some way. She slid her hand along the wall, but then, without meaning to, she pushed one block straight through. The whole chamber shook dreadfully. Dust and stones and all sorts fell from the ceiling. The archaeologists began to panic slightly, as they all put their arms over their heads trying to protect themselves from falling stone. The wall began to move upwards. As it moved into the ceiling, a bright orange light wafted from the other side, and spilled into the dark passageway in which they were all gathered.

Finally, the whole wall had ascended into the ceiling and revealed an extremely large room. It was amazing. Katie-Anne just stood there staring at it, with Adam and the archaeologists gazing struck dumb over her shoulders. Inside the thrilling room was another statue of the Sphinx, apart from this statue was a lot smaller and had not succumbed to the tragedy of weathering and eroding as there was no hole in the ceiling for wind or rain to trespass. The Sphinx was perfect in every way. It had the beautiful and slender face of a fair lady, its paws were long and curved and it had the so-called scorpion tail, quivering powerfully above its back. The statue looked almost alive. The Sphinx lay on a small island surrounded by a moat filled with water. Stalactites as long as telephone polls hung from the ceiling. The room was filled with torches lit by an orange flame and they hung on wooden brackets all over walls. Finally, right on the very quiver on the scorpion's tail on the Sphinx hung a small golden box. It shone elegantly in the light of the orange flames. Katie-Anne noticed on the far wall hung a tablet. The same tablet, in fact that she had the picture of; the picture in the folder that had landed on her desk and started all this off in the first place. She looked at it gleefully for a moment then thought of something. If she was supposedly the first person to find an entrance into the Sphinx, how did someone manage to take a picture of the tablet? This must mean that someone must have found his or her way into the Sphinx before she had. This was all getting very confusing. While she was thinking to herself, the archaeologists had swarmed around the chamber like locusts and began examining every inch of it. Adam however, did not go examining the chamber, but stood behind Katie-Anne. When she noticed this, she turned around.

"See, this project wasn't a waste of time after all!" Katie-Anne gloated.

"Yeah, yeah what ever." At that very moment, an almighty eruption occurred. The force was so much so, that Katie-Anne was lifted off her feet and thrown three feet backwards back into the dark passage. Katie-Anne looked up. Her archaeologists were lying scattered on the ground and Adam was lying in a heap just in front of her. She got up quickly and went back into the chamber to see what had caused the explosion. The golden box from the tail of the Sphinx was lying open at the Sphinx's paw and the archaeologist that had opened it was lying beside it, apparently unconscious. A strong light was coming from the golden box. Then, streaks of multicoloured light ripped away from the light and exited through the door. It stopped after a few minutes, and the golden lid fell from the ceiling and landed back onto the box with a loud 'THUMP'. A few seconds after the lid had landed back onto the box, a light soft purring voice spoke through the chamber.

"You could not possibly know what danger and wrath you have unleashed upon the world!" it said. Katie-Anne and the archaeologists looked at the source of the voice, which was coming from the statue in the middle of the moat. Atop the statue, was a real living, breathing Sphinx. Its beautiful lion body was a golden yellow with a tint of red and a blush red scorpion tail protruded from where its normal tail usually went. Its head was the head of the most beautiful, stunning woman any man could lay eyes on.

"So it begins!"

Chapter 5
Sphinx the Guardian

Every eye in the whole chamber was upon this vast, peculiar creature. No one seemed to remember how to speak or move.

"The monsters of mythology have risen again," the Sphinx said, with an air of grave annoyance in its voice. It pounced from the statue of itself and landed cat-like on the other side of the moat.

"Your, you, your- a sphinx!" Katie-Anne murmured disbelievingly, looking at the Sphinx like she had not looked like anything else before.

"Yes, you are quite right, I am a Sphinx. The Sphinx was not just a statue in the middle of a desert you know. Oh no, the Sphinx came before the statue. As Sphinxes, me and my sisters-"

"-there are more of you!?" Adam interrupted; also looking at the Sphinx like it was some bizarre dream. The Sphinx didn't seem to mind at all that Adam had rudely interfered with her speech. On the contrary, she was smiling broadly at him.

"Yes, that is correct; I am not the only living Sphinx. In total there are five of us. We are guardians of the Earth's four primary elements. Much more importantly, we also guard an aspect of Earth. I guard the hot, gruelling deserts. My other sisters guard the oceans, the mountains, the skies, and the forests."

"Does that mean there is more than one statue of, well, you?" Adam asked curiously. The Sphinx's smile melted away immediately and gloom seemed to settle upon her, as if she was remembering something she would rather forget.

"No, just the statue in the desert. You see, there is only one statue because I was the only one foolish enough to get caught," the Sphinx said miserably.

"What do you mean?" Katie-Anne gabbled.

"I suppose it all begins when my four sisters and I were first sent to guard the Earth. When my sisters and I came to live on the planet, human kind did not exist yet. We lived for thousands of years, trying to keep the natural balance of the world in place. Eventually, the desert in Egypt (to you the Sahara desert) was inhabited by the first Egyptians. The Ancient Egyptians. When we were sent to Earth, we were told that under no circumstances were we to be allowed to be seen by anything that had a superior intelligence to other creatures. But, unluckily, one day I was flying high above Egypt. I got caught in a sandstorm. The storm blew me away and I landed on the sand, right on the edge of an Egyptian town. The Egyptians saw me and kept trying to get close to me. I had failed; I had let intelligent eyes set their sight upon me. I was the only one caught. The Egyptians built a statue of me and for some reason they saw me as a God. They kept offering sacrifices to me, like their other Gods, and the people they killed were buried inside my statue, as you saw. My ageing grandfather was extremely ashamed of what had happened. He had had enough scandals in his life and this one was one too many. The shock killed him. The possessions he left behind were one of the most powerful and valuable that had ever been made. They needed to be guarded."

"Who was your grandfather?" Katie-Anne asked curiously.

"My grandfather was one of the four most powerful beings. He was one of the first creatures to ever live and take a resemblance to human form. He was called Poseidon, great ruler of the-"

"Poseidon!?" Adam exploded excitedly, again interrupting the Sphinx's speech. "Isn't he that elderly merman?"

"You are correct young sir. After he died, things became unbalanced. My grandfather was one of the four powers of the world.

Many thousands of years ago, the world was roamed by what you people now call today 'mythical' animals. And when my grandfather died, it was these animals that went out of control. So, in the end, my sisters and I decided to seal away all the mythical animals and attempt to restore the balance. We contained them in that golden box. And to stop our grandfather's powerful possessions ever getting into evil hands, we devised a way of locking them away."

"But, if mythical creatures once roamed our planet, then surely they would have left some trace behind?" Katie-Anne asked thoughtfully. Yet again the Sphinx smiled, as if it liked being asked questions in which she gave long-winded answers.

"But they did. People who lived in the time of these animals drew pictures about them, wrote about them, told stories which people these days think are just legendary. Unlike all the normal animals however, they left no physical trace behind once they died. No bones, no fossils, no DNA, nothing. Because people only had pictures to rely on, the animals became 'mythical' and were never known to have existed." Silence followed these words. Katie-Anne felt that she had just discovered a new dimension of the Earth that had not been looked into before- the dimension with the Sphinx in, and the one without.

"Where are Poseidon's possessions?" Adam asked hungrily.

"You have to possess all the five keys to get them. My sisters and I have a key each. However, we will not be so stupid and blind to give them away willingly. You have to solve a riddle from each of us before we will burden you with our keys. They are not the average riddles one would expect, but complicated mind numbing riddles you couldn't possibly imagine.

"So we have to solve riddles. So, if we successfully decode your riddle, we can get your key?" asked Katie-Anne.

"That is correct," replied the Sphinx.

"So, can we hear your riddle?" Adam asked nervously.

"I'm sorry, but I cannot let you hear my riddle first. My reasons are my own. You must find my sisters and gain all of their keys before I can let you except mine," the Sphinx replied.

"Where will we find the other four Sphinxes?" Katie-Anne asked desperately.

"That answer I can give. You should start at the Amazon Rain forest. There you will find your first prize. Now you must go, hurry," replied the

Sphinx, with a tone of impatience in her voice. Sensing this, the archaeologists scrambled for the door. Katie-Anne was finally the only one left. She was just about to exit, when she turned back around to ask another question.

"What will happen to the world now the creatures have been unleashed?" Katie-Anne asked worriedly.

"Great pandemonium," replied the Sphinx gravely, the smile vanishing completely off her face.

"How do we recapture them?" Katie-Anne asked anxiously.

"You must first unlock all of Poseidon's possessions. There will be one possession that will react with the box and reabsorb all the creatures back in." With that, Katie-Anne swivelled around and left the Chamber. Adam was waiting for her in the dark passage. All the others had gone on.

"What do we do now?" he asked in the most frightened yet excited voice that Katie-Anne had ever heard him speak in.

"We send the archaeologists home. They can't help us anymore; they've done enough already. There is no point in gambling their lives," replied Katie-Anne sternly.

"We should have taken the Mystery Man's advice and abandoned the project," Adam whispered sulkily.

"Why?" said Katie-Anne sounding surprised.

"Hmmm, let's think shall we. We've broken the balance of the world, we've unleashed a pack of monsters that were never thought to exist and we have to find a way of returning them. But apart from that I couldn't possibly think why we would have continued with this stupid trip," Adam said sarcastically and bitterly.

"But that can all be fixed-"

"-FIXED!! What chance do we have? How on earth are we ever going to find the remaining four Sphinxes while trying to get past a pack of ravenous supernatural beasts? We should end this project while we still have our lives."

"Don't you understand!? This is no longer some stupid expedition! This has become the fate of the world, and as it is our fault it has happened, we are the ones responsible for fixing it.

Their discussion had led them back to the entrance of the Sphinx. As they emerged from the hole, the strange block slid back into place. The archaeologists were slumped around the Land Rovers looking scared and talking in frightened voices.

"Thank you for your co-operation everyone! You have all been an asset to this project. You are now all free to return to your homes. I will organise a plane home for you all tomorrow. One more thing! You will not tell anyone what transpired here. Go." The workers didn't need telling twice. They quickly stumbled into the vehicles and drove off, until only one Rover remained for Katie-Anne and Adam.

"I think while you're booking for a flight for the workers to fly home tomorrow, you should also book two tickets to the Amazon," Adam said casually, looking at the desert in front of him.

"Does this mean your coming then?" Katie-Anne asked hopefully.

"Course it does. I can't let you do this alone, can I?" he replied, a smile appearing on his face.

*

The day's surprises for Katie-Anne were not yet complete. When they arrived back at their Hotel, Katie-Anne found her laptop back on her bed. She stared at it uncertainly at first. She noticed a note next to it, which read, *"You'll be needing this."*

Katie-Anne quickly logged herself on and booked all the tickets that she needed for the workers and for her and Adam. While she was on her laptop, she turned on her Television, hoping to catch the Arabic news. She couldn't understand the language they were speaking in, but she could certainly tell what was going on. It looks like the creatures that they had released had been appearing everywhere. She stared out of her window, gazing at the sunset and thinking of the dangerous new adventure she was sure to follow.

Chapter 6
Women of the Wood

A few days after the disastrous trip to the Sphinx statue, Katie-Anne and Adam were ready to travel to Brazil, and into the Amazon Rainforest just like the Sphinx advised them. However, the past few days were not unexciting. A winged yellow turtle that was obviously from the Golden Box and a mythical animal attacked the Hotel, but Katie-Anne didn't recognise it as an animal she had ever studied.

The day after, the sky turned extremely stormy as some of the clouds appeared to have come to life and began vanquishing Egypt with many heavy showers that the country was not used to seeing. Katie-Anne knew she was one of only a few that could put a stop to this dire mess, but it didn't make it any easier when she pondered about what saving the world would involve.

*

The aeroplane journey was also in some way eventful. Basically, out of fear of seeing some ghastly creature from god knows what era, all the passengers had closed the blinds on their windows. But the journey was a little more exciting than that. In the duration of the journey, Katie-Anne had become quite thirsty and needed a drink.

"Excuse me!" she called to a passing air attendant who just walked by carting a rickety trolley. The steward turned around, and as Katie-Anne gazed upon him, she lost the will to talk. It wasn't that she fancied the man, but she was a little overcome with shock because she swore that she had seen this man somewhere before. He wore a light blue shirt and dark pinstriped trousers as his uniform. An 'Arabian Transports' badge was fixed to his shirt. His face was slightly tanned and he had rather small brown eyes. One long eyebrow grew its way above his eyelids. His hair fell back into a neat ponytail behind him.

"Yes, madam?" he replied politely. Katie-Anne stared at him.

"Um, yes, um, could I have…a drink of orange please?" she stuttered in reply.

"Right away!" replied the man. The man carted his trolley off into the plane lounge and then came back moments later carrying a glass of juice. As he handed it to Katie-Anne, he glared at her for a brief moment and then walked away to serve someone else. As soon as he left, Katie-Anne bent over and whispered in Adam's ear.

"I swear I've seen him before somewhere, I just don't remember where. There's something familiar about him, I just can't remember where I've seen him."

"May be you know him in another life," replied Adam sarcastically; flicking a page in the magazine he was reading. Katie-Anne glowered at him.

"Will you be serious!? I know I've him somewhere before, I know it!" she whispered frantically.

"No, you're just being paranoid. Stop being so suspicious and enjoy the flight, as we wont be able to relax a lot once we arrive. You might have seen him at the airport before we took off. Or you might have seen him somewhere else. There could be a hundred and one places. Or, most sensibly, you haven't ever seen him before and he probably reminds you of a person you know or knew," Adam suggested.

"Stop being so obtuse. I've seen him more than once, but where I don't know." She engaged herself in silent thought, desperately trying to think where she had seen the man before. After a few minutes she gave up and thought that Adam was probably right. She probably was just being too paranoid because of the excitement and nervous feelings floating about in her body like a surge of adrenalin at the thought of what she would likely encounter in the very near future.

"Anyway, don't you think you should be spending more of your time worrying about all the dangerous creatures that have been reintroduced back onto the world and threatening world peace; rather than deciding whether you claim to have seen some man on an aeroplane from your past?" Adam said airily.

"Well, I'm glad that you're taking a positive approach!" Katie-Anne replied sarcastically, raising her voice slightly and glaring at his magazine, as though it to had contradicted her thoughts.

"Just forget I said anything," Adam replied as he buried his face amongst the magazine.

*

The rest of the flight past fairly swiftly. They landed in Rio de Janeiro and borrowed a car to drive to their Hotel. They were planning to drive to the Amazon in a few hours, but first they needed to make sure they had all the essentials and any equipment they might need just in case an emergency arose.

*

After they had reached their desired location on the outskirts of the forest, they trekked into the rainforest. The trees went higher than they ever imagined, sometimes their canopies blocking the sunlight from passing through. The further they walked, the more different and amazing sounds they began to hear. They could hear at least fifteen different birdcalls echoing around the forest as they talked and squabbled with each other over food. They walked further in; and the further they got, the thicker and the taller trees began to appear, until eventually no sun could penetrate through the branches at all.

"Do you know where you're going?" Adam asked after an hour and a half of walking.

"Not really, no," replied Katie-Anne as she just kept on walking through, hoping to find something that would make their trip worthwhile. They walked for five more minutes when Adam eventually stopped to take out his compass. He was just beginning to look at it when he heard a large twig snap loudly behind him. They both turned around quickly, only to find something unwelcoming. A large terrible beast stood before them. The monster had a pale body that seemed to resemble a cross between a lion and a goat. It's fore legs where the legs of a lion but its hind legs appeared to be the legs of a goat. The creature did not have one head like all other living animals you would come across, this one had two, one of a lion and one of a goat. Each head had canine teeth that grew out of their jaws and grew further than their chins. They had vicious, murderous red eyes, which plainly told them it wanted food, and that Katie-Anne and Adam were first on the menu. The monster had a tail like most other animals, but it wasn't a tail you would usually come across. This beast had a tail of a purple snake, which hissed menacingly behind the creature. Every time the snake tail took breath small flames erupted out of the snake's mouth. The terrible fiend took a step towards them, and Katie-Anne and Adam in turn took a step back. Being a mythologist, Katie-Anne recognised the beast at once.

"What-what is that?" Adam said calmly, not daring to take his eyes of the beast, but looking at it as if he had just walked into pit full of his worst fears.

"It-I do believe it's a…Chimera," Katie-Anne replied, also looking directly at the beast.

"Oh, a Chimera, well that's nice to know!" Adam replied trying to make a joke of it all. They both kept on creeping away slowly, but every step they took, the Chimera took some too.

"How're we supposed to get away from it?" Adam asked hopefully.

"I don't know," Katie-Anne replied fearfully.

"Well, didn't you do some kind of report on them? You should know quite a bit about them, shouldn't you?" Adam asked.

"Is it really the time to discuss that?" Katie-Anne said in a slightly louder voice.

"What do you think about running?" Adam suggested.

"We will never make it. Chimera's are built for their speed." But then, a thought struck Katie-Anne. This beast wanted food, that's why it was attacking them. She had a loaf of bread in her bag. If the heads were hungry, they would surely squabble over any small morsel of food.

"I have an idea," she said. She slowly took off her rucksack, and took out the bread. Both Chimera heads averted their attention towards the bread and gazed at it greedily. They began sniffing the air and growling. Katie-Anne threw it into the air towards the Chimera, and the creature dived for it.

"RUN!" she yelled. Adam didn't need telling twice. Katie-Anne glanced back to see what the Chimera was doing. The heads were fighting with each other, as the goat head tried to pull the bread out of the lion heads mouth. Since Katie-Anne wasn't looking where she was going, she ran headfirst into a tree, and a strange emerald green branch fell down. The branch was shining brilliantly.

"Are you alright?" Adam asked, trying to get her up quickly.

"Yeah." She took the branch and they kept on running. Then, the Chimera leaped above their heads and landed in front of them.

"Oh no, this isn't good," Adam murmured. The Chimera was growling angrily as it approached them. "Any more ideas?" he asked hopefully.

"No. It was nice knowing you Adam," said Katie-Anne as she stared death in the face, literally.

"Yeah, same here," replied Adam. But then, out of nowhere, a strange mystical humming started. All other sounds in the forest were vanquished and this humming was the dominating sound. The humming was beautiful, it was like something Katie-Anne and Adam had never heard before. They felt relaxed with this humming, as if all their worries and problems no longer mattered. The ground began to excrete strange green illuminated particles, which rose into the air and began to form together into what appeared to be an orb made of green light. It got bigger as more of the strange green particles were added to it. It was just a guess, but Katie-Anne had a feeling it was something to do with the humming.

"What's happening?" Adam asked, as the green particles floated by him. With each passing moment, the humming got louder, and the louder the humming became, the more of the green particles started to appear and add to the ball. Both of the Chimera heads bared their fangs at the orb angrily, as if it saw the orb as some kind of threat. The snake tail curled over the Chimera's back. It took one almighty breath and hurled an enormous flamethrower from its mouth towards the orb. The flames just curled away from the orb, not affecting it in the slightest. The Chimera backed away angrily, hissing at the orb.

"What should we do?" Adam asked impatiently.

"Just stay where you are for a moment." Katie-Anne didn't know what was about to happen, but she felt as though she could trust the green orb.

Once the green orb of energy had roughly reached the size of a small house, the strange sparkling green dust stopped lifting from the ground and disappeared. The humming did not stop however, and suddenly, in the forest in front of them, came some of the most bizarre creatures that Katie-Anne and Adam had ever seen. They appeared to be walking trees that resembled women. Instead of skin, they were layered with dark, polished smooth wood of some kind. They didn't have red lips like people do; their lips were made of tree bark. They didn't have hair, they had small branches growing off their heads that blossomed into plump leaves and a lovely white flower that Katie-Anne and Adam had never seen before. Their eyes were human enough, apart from the sclerotic of the eyes were tinted green, and all of their pupils were dark brown in colour. All of the tree women wore long velvety green gowns that swept the forest floor. All of them had their hands clasped together in front of them as if they were praying, and the soft humming seemed to be coming from them. They huddled into a tighter group, and a band of what appeared to be floating green beads hovered around them. There were about eight of the tree women in all.

The woman right at the front of the group had a crown made of silver on her head. She raised her hands gently over her head and green orb turned quickly a blush burning white. One of the women who was closer to Katie-Anne and Adam, broke away from the others and swept swiftly towards Katie-Anne and Adam.

"You must back away from here quickly," it said in a very soft echoing voice.

"What, umm I mean, who are you?" asked Katie-Anne staring transfixed at the woman in front of her.

"This is not the right time to discuss it now. You must go, quickly!" it replied. She grabbed Katie-Anne's hand and hurried her away. Adam followed closely behind them. They ran behind a tree about fifty yards away. They could still see the Chimera. It was looking at the tree woman furiously. It kept breathing fire at them but the hovering green beads protected them.

"If that fire hits them, they will be toasted," Katie-Anne said anxiously.

"Don't worry, it will take more than fire from a Chimera to penetrate through that force field," replied the tree woman.

The tree women stopped humming and the orb let out small rays of light. The tree woman who had raised her hands above her head brought them swishing down. The orb came down as her hands did, straight at the Chimera. The Chimera was just about to leap away when, too late, the orb had struck. The explosion was incredible. Anything that was in the orbs path was ripped away from the ground and was either dissolved through the pressure of the orb or blown away. Katie-Anne, Adam and the tree woman ducked as ground and plants flew above their heads and landed pell-mell around them. When they got up, they saw the Chimera lying injured on the ground, a few feet away from where the orb had stuck. It got up onto its legs gingerly and limped away. The hovering beads around the women vanished and they walked down towards Katie-Anne and Adam. The other tree woman went to join her group.

"Who are you?" Katie-Anne asked for the second time.

"We are Shee Nymphs," replied the woman wearing the crown. "We protect stragglers in the forests in which we live. Tell we, what brings you into the heart of such an unsafe forest?"

"We are on quest to find the five Sphinxes and seal away all the monsters back into the Golden Box," replied Adam. The Nymphs broke out into a horrified chatter as soon as he finished talking.

"How could you possibly know about the Golden box or the Sphinx," said the head Nymph horrified.

"It all started as an expedition to find an entrance into the statue of the Sphinx in Egypt. We found it. One of the men on our project opened the box and let all of the mythical creatures out. We are now on a journey to put things right, and the Sphinx of Egypt told us to start here," Adam told.

"Is that where you come from as well, the Golden box?" Katie-Anne asked "And how is it that you can speak English?" The Nymph considered her for a moment.

"You are indeed correct on guessing our origin. We indeed came from the Golden Box. All 'mythical creatures' as you call them are animals made by the sovereign. We can speak any language that we like. Going back to the previous point, I can already foretell that on a mission as dangerous and as important as this you will not last more than a few days. If it were not for our passing, you would already be Chimera fodder. You will need more than human intelligence to complete this journey."

"What do you mean? So your saying that it is impossible for us to complete this quest without powers like yours?" Adam asked anxiously.

"May be. I sense something special about you, as if you were born for this duty, no one else. So what can we do?" pondered the Nymph. It was only then that Katie-Anne remembered about the weird branch that she found when she was running from the Chimera.

"Excuse me." The Nymphs looked at her. "When we were running from the Chimera, I found this. Could you tell me what it is?" she asked. Katie-Anne handed the branch to the Nymphs. The head Nymph stared at it with wide eyes.

"Could it be!?" said the Nymph disbelievingly. She opened her free hand. The same sparkly green energy that made the orb appeared in her hands and formed into a real solid thick book. Katie-Anne could tell it was very old. The cover and spine was made of leather and the pages were yellowing and rippled. There was something inscribed in gold symbols on the front cover. The Nymph opened up the thick volume and looked at something. "It is!" she said, looking at the branch in awe. "You've discovered an Elementite."

"What on earth is an Elementite?" Katie-Anne asked curiously.

"You do know about the four primary elements of the world don't you?" asked the Nymph.

"You mean water, fire, air and earth?" Adam replied.

"Yes, that's it. Well, sometime unknown to anyone, many objects were crafted. The objects contained a power of one of these elements. Now each object had a special power unique to that element that could not be learned any other way. Somehow, all the objects were separated and scattered all over the world. These objects were called Elementites."

"So what Elementite is that, and what's with the book that you're holding?" Adam asked

"This book is a record of all the known Elementites. It shows you what the Elementite looks like and describes what power it bestows."

"So, what element does that branch contain?" Katie-Anne asked curiously.

"According to this book, this Elementite contains an earthen power called 'Twig Ensnare'. Of course, you can't use the power of the Elementites unless you have the power of the element yourself. We would be able to use it because we all posses the power of earth."

"So its pretty useless to us then?" Adam said disappointedly.

"Not quite. There is a way you can learn the power of earth," said the Nymph smiling at the two of them.

"How?" asked Katie-Anne.

"A creature or being that controls an elemental power can transfer that power to whomever he or she wishes. But, the power will only transfer if the being transferring the power has a valid reason for doing so."

"So, if you don't have a valid reason, the power would not transfer to us?" asked Adam. "You make it sound like the elemental powers have wills of their own."

"You should not be so quick to judge something you know so little about. The elemental powers are the most sacred of all treasures. They have powers so great that they could reform the Earth into an entirely new world. Everything you see is a combination of these four elements."

"So, will you try to pass on your earthen powers over to use?" Katie-Anne asked excitedly.

"You will need a power such as this to complete your quest. However, we understand that we cannot force our hand on this. It is up to you to decide."

"Of course!" replied Katie-Anne.

"Definitely!" Adam said. The head Nymph clicked her finger. The ground beneath Katie-Anne and Adam began to glow green and the same sparkling green energy used to create the orb appeared around them. The energy hovered around them. They were both lifted a few inches above the ground and the green energy began to insert into Katie-Anne and Adam. Katie-Anne could feel a weird sensation in her body, like sand running through her veins instead of blood. It wasn't an unpleasant feeling, but it did make feel a little weary. After a few moments, it was all over and Katie-Anne and Adam dropped back onto the ground and the green energy disappeared.

"A gift from us to you," spoke the Nymph. "You have to power to control the ground and anything on it as you will. You must use this power wisely. You must not use this power for anything that is dishonourable. If you betray such a promise, you will find that we will personally hunt you down. And one more thing"- the Nymph handed the book on Elementites to Katie-Anne. "You will benefit more from this than we will. We wish you the best of luck on your quest and hope that it is successful."

"Wait! How do you use this power, we know nothing about it."

"The power of the elemental will guide you, don't worry."

"But, if we seal the mythical animals back into the Golden box, doesn't that mean you will be sealed back as well?" Adam interrupted changing the topic. The Shee Nymph smiled.

"Yes it does. But, the time of the mythical animals has long passed. We are no longer needed here, and as you see, when we are here when there are other civilizations, the two worlds clash and only one must be stopped. It is the mythical animals that must go. We have roamed the Earth long enough. It is time we step down and let others take our place. Do not let this fact distract you. You must lock us in the box." She smiled at them. "Farewell to you both!" All of the Nymphs raised a hand in front of them in farewell then their bodies turned into the same green sparkling energy and they were gone.

Chapter 7
Knight-Mare from the Sand

Katie-Anne opened out her palm expecting something to happen. Slowly, a foot high oak tree sprouted in the palm of her hand. When she clenched her hand, the oak disappeared in the same sparkling green energy.

"This power-it's amazing!" she gasped, staring at her hand.

"It's unbelievable!" replied Adam in awe. Neither of them wanted to continue going, they just wanted to test their new powers. After about ten minutes, they decided it was time to press on and they walked even further into the forest, every now and again staring at the hands still ecstatic about their powers.

"Do you actually know where you're going?" Adam asked after an hour of walking.

"No. But I suppose we have to go in deeper. We'll find something eventually, I'm sure of it!" replied Katie-Anne trying to convince herself.

No sooner had they taken five more steps than their newfound powers were put to the test. At first, they heard a very unusual sound. It sounded like a large pack of dogs nearby.

"What is that noise, dogs?" Adam asked he looked around for the source of the noise.

"It can't be. Dogs don't live in this forest. And it sounds like far too many dogs for them to have come with people," replied Katie-Anne, also looking around. The sound of the dogs was getting nearer.

"You don't think its another mythical animal do you?" Adam asked wearily.

"As a matter of fact, I do," but there was a tone of utmost fear in her voice. "There is only one mythical animal that makes a sound like that, and is feared amongst all other animals. I just hope this sound isn't coming from the creature I'm thinking of." As she finished talking, the creature making the noise bounced in front of them, but this one differed from the Chimera. It was a lot fouler than the Chimera. Katie-Anne looked upon it, her worst fears realised. But as the creature stopped running, the sound of the pack of dogs ended.

"Is, that the animal that you were talking about?" Adam asked looking at the creature, terrified.

"It is. It's known as the Questing Beast, a beast with a leopard's body and a serpent's head, just like this animal. It spends all of its life looking for water, to try and quench its unquenchable thirst. As is runs looking for water, its belly emits the sound of a thousand angry hounds," said Katie-Anne.

"Why were you so afraid of it, if it's 'questing' for water, it wont hurt is, will it?"

"You don't understand. This beast won't just drink water, it will drink any liquid it can find. Imagine being stuck in the Sahara Desert in the middle of the summer on the hottest day with no water. This is how this beast feels every second of its life. It will drink anything, including our blood." The Questing Beats leaped onto Adam and pinned him to the floor. Katie-Anne picked up a branch from the floor and threw it at the beast as hard as she could. The beast turned its serpent head round and decided to go for Katie-Anne instead. Katie-Anne screamed and stuck her hands in front of her face trying to protect herself. The same sparkling green energy from before erupted from her hands and formed into a large thick brown vine that struck the beast to the floor; and then it disappeared. Katie-Anne gasped and looked at her hands, looking completely dumbstruck at what she had accomplished. The beast got back up to its feet steadily and its eyes narrowed. It whacked one of its front paws on the ground and the rocks and stones lifted and formed into about two dozen small dogs, each about the size of a large pumpkin; that lunged for Katie-Anne. Somehow, as she saw the stone dogs running towards her, she somehow knew what to do, like her new powers were guiding her. She directed her hand towards the ground and in the same sparkling green energy; an enormous stone spire erupted from the ground. It formed into some sort of lance and cleaved through all the dogs and struck the Questing Beast. The beast got up for the second time and sprinted for Katie-Anne, the sound of ravenous hounds starting again.

"Use the Elementite!" Adam shouted over the racket. Katie-Anne lifted her Radiant Branch into the air. Branches erupted from the ground in front of her and curled themselves around the Questing beast, tangling him up and lifting him high into the air. It kept trying to bite through the vines, but to no avail.

"I think we should get out of here in case it manages to find its way out somehow," said Adam. He grabbed Katie-Anne's hand and hurried forward. They suddenly emerged upon a clearing with no trees whatsoever. However, there was a huge rock formation, covered in thick chucks of ivy and bushes. The rock formation had crumbled and eroded in many places, and the floor around the rock formation was littered with large rocks that had peeled away from the mother rock.

The rock formation went too high for Katie-Anne and Adam to see the top of the formation as it disappeared into the clouds at a certain height. However the rock formation had an extraordinary formation. Encrusted quite close to the base of the rock formation, near to where Katie-Anne was standing, was a woman's face, carved out of what appeared to be gold. It sparkled slightly through the little light that had managed to penetrate through the dense canopy of trees that Katie-Anne and Adam had just walked through.

"What's this all about?" Adam whispered curiously to Katie-Anne.

"I'm not sure," Katie-Anne replied. Katie-Anne took a few steps closer towards the face. She looked at it for a moment.

"This face seems to remind me of someone," She said at last. Adam snorted.

"Please Kate, not this again. Every time you see something or someone they always remind you of someone," Adam grunted. Katie-Anne glared at him, and then chose to look back at the golden face.

"Just do me one favour. Come and have a look for yourself and see if it reminds *you* of anyone," replied Katie-Anne. Adam rolled his eyes and walked forwards casually and looked at the face. But he didn't give the answer he himself thought he might give.

"Kate, I think you're right, I think this face reminds me of someone too."

"I've figured out who it is," she said impressively.

"Well? Who is it then?"

"It's the face of the Sphinx. This must be where we need to be."

"I think your right. But, what are we meant to do now we are here, climb the rock?" Adam asked anxiously looking into the sky where the formation disappeared into the clouds.

"No, I don't think so." Katie-Anne moved slowly towards the formation. She stretched out her hand and touched the golden face. It was cold against her palm. Katie-Anne realised the eyes of the face consisted of emeralds. She touched them, half hoping for something dramatic to happen. Nothing did. Katie-Anne withdrew her hand.

"So now what?" Adam asked.

"Be quite for a moment I'm trying to think." As she said this, the emerald eyes on the face flared and the formation shook angrily. Rocks fell hither and thither from the top of the formation.

"Katie-Anne, watch out!" Adam dived for Katie-Anne just in time as a boulder struck where she was standing moments before. The mouth of the golden face slipped open revealing a large dark hole. The tremor stopped and the last few smaller stones rained down upon them.

"Should we enter?" Adam asked nervously.

"I don't know. And I certainly don't fancy trying to squeeze in there," she replied, looking into the dark hole. As she spoke, sand began pouring out of the hole of the mouth and piled onto the forest floor.

After about twenty seconds the sand stopped and wafted as if it was caught in a breeze. The sand began to collapse upon itself before forming into a shape, a shape similar to that of a human. When the sand was satisfied with its posture and shape it solidified into stone. The creature it took the appearance of was most bizarre. It looked like a fifteen ft knight with deliberate mistakes. Its helm had one large horn protruding out of the forehead that curved up slightly at the end. Its arms didn't wield weapons; they were weapons. Its left arm was a sword and its right arm was a lance. The knight stood upon a huge shield. The knight appeared to be made from a dark metamorphic rock. As Katie-Anne gazed upon the knight, she saw something shining within the sword. Directly in the centre of the sword appeared to be a clear orb. Inside the orb there appeared to be lots of different coloured sands, which shone brightly.

Meanwhile, the knight whipped his sword arm to the ground and the shield rose into the air a few feet with the knight on it. The knight raised its lance arm and charged straight towards Katie-Anne and Adam. They both dived towards the ground. Katie-Anne felt a sharp breeze pass over her head as the knight drifted over her. Adam stood up. He threw his right arm in front of him and a flurry of large daisy heads went pelting towards the knight. The knight smashed them out of the way with its sword arm and they went spinning off and cut into a tree bark like throwing stars. The knight went soaring towards Adam. Katie-Anne stood up and used the Radiant Branch. Branches and vines erupted from the ground and made their way towards the knight. The knight brought down his sword arm and sliced threw the branches. The knight's horn began to glow blue, which emitted a pack of rocky spikes that tore their way towards Katie-Anne and Adam. Adam sent up a large hydrangea bush to block them. The knight raised his sword arm into the air. The orb began to glow and storm of multicoloured sand tore threw the hydrangea bush and took down Katie-Anne and Adam. Katie-Anne stood up gingerly and whipped her right hand to her side. A long green whip covered in thorns and red roses appeared at her side with a snap. She whipped it at the knight and it caught him in the middle. The knight was throw off his shield and smacked into the tree that bore the daisies. The shield went soaring off like a wild Frisbee and cut clean through a mahogany tree like scissors on paper.

The knight got steadily to its feet. Adam clicked his fingers and from his hand, apples went pelting towards the knight like pellets. The knight fell down again, but was unable to get up because it didn't have any hands to lift itself up with. Katie-Anne clapped her wrists together and opened up her hands. A large cauliflower formed and launched from her hands. As it hit the knight it exploded. Bits of black rock flew everywhere and the knight's sword arm landed directly in front of them. The knight itself lay on the ground in shambles, defeated. Both Katie-Anne and Adam looked at the sword arm and at the orb inside. As they touched the arm it dissolved and left only the orb behind. Adam picked it up. The different coloured sands inside shone beautifully.

"Is this another Elementite?" Adam asked excitedly, examining the orb.

"I'll check," replied Katie-Anne. She took out the thick volume that the Shee Nymphs had given them and flicked through it. "Yes, look here! It's called the Planetary Sand. Apparently it contains sand or dust from every planet in this solar system. It contains a power called 'Space dust'. That must be what that knight used on us."

"So we have one each now. You have the Radiant Branch, and I have the Planetary Sand. Are you sure this Elementite contains a power of earth so that I can use it?"

"Yes, it is an Elementite of Earth." But as they talked about the Elementite, the mountain shook yet again, sending more showers of rocks down upon them. The mouth of the golden face opened even wider, this time revealing a hole large enough to fit a fairly big Water Buffalo.

"This is it!" whispered Adam excitedly.

"Don't get your hopes up. Hopefully there are no more monsters in this thing waiting for us. This is our first day of the quest and we've already had to fight three monsters," replied Katie-Anne peering into the dark hole.

"Well, ladies first," Adam inquired from behind Katie-Anne. She glowered at him.

"A right gentleman, aren't you?" she replied sarcastically. She stuck her head through the hole and followed through with her body. At once, she went zooming down a long twisted tunnel that felt a lot like a water slide in a horror house. All Katie-Anne could see was darkness. At last she saw a circle of light in front of her and she went shooting out of the end and landed with a soft 'flump' on the ground. Adam charged out after her and landed just a bit in front of her. They both gazed around the room that they had intruded upon. In the centre of the room grew an enormous tree, which grew high into the mountaintop. When Katie-Anne looked up, she saw that there was no top to the mountain. Instead, it opened out into the sky, and the tree, with its thousands of branches grew well out of the mountain.

Strange blue birds flittered and sang around the tree. The ground was compiled of short, even grass. A large pond filled the corner of the room and big purple fish with green wings kept diving in and out like dolphins. Smaller trees gathered randomly around the room. Katie-Anne and Adam saw that these trees were the home to strange yellowish monkeys that had small tusks growing out of their jaw. As they looked around, they heard a loud bird call that sounded as if it came from an eagle.

"This is magical!" Adam murmured.

"This is beautiful!" Katie-Anne gasped.

"This is the Jungle Shrine," came a voice from their left. A Sphinx stood there, looking exactly the same as the one they met in Egypt, apart from this one was very slightly tinted green in colour.

"Looks like my Stone Knight has lost a battle at last." The Sphinx shook its head. "And how may I help you?" it asked politely, smiling at the shocked expressions fixed upon the faces of Katie-Anne and Adam. Katie-Anne and Adam just stood there, trying to believe they had just come face to face with the forest Sphinx.

Chapter 8
The Tragonzite and the Cave

"You're the Forest Sphinx," Katie-Anne murmured.

"Yes I am. But I think, more importantly, who are you, are how did you come to be here?" the Sphinx asked, sounding slightly impressed.

"Oh, I am called Katie-Anne Springwood, and this is my friend, Adam Heart," Katie-Anne replied, talking as though she had met someone highly important, like the Queen. "We were sent here by your sister, the Sphinx of Egypt." The Sphinx's face flashed.

"Really, and why is that then?" the Sphinx asked, her voice becoming dangerously high.

"Well, we found the entrance into the statue of the Sphinx and we accidentally opened the Golden Box," Adam spoke. The Sphinx closed her eyes, as though hoping what she was hearing wasn't true. "We wanted to put the world right again, and we heard we could only do that by collecting the five keys that you and your sisters possess."

"Do you know what cataclysmal you have caused by letting the mythical animals free?" replied the Sphinx, opening her eyes at last.

"We know; the balance of the world has been upset because the time of the mythical animals ended long ago. That's why we are here, to sort it out," Adam responded impatiently.

"Oh no my friends. An even worse threat than that has been revealed. My father, the Manticore."

"What's so bad about this Manticore? Surely it's just like all other...wait, did you say your father!?" replied Adam, sounding quite shocked.

"My father was an evil man you know. He left us at birth. My mother never had the chance to tell us why because she died shortly after giving birth to us. When my dear grandfather died, we were in turmoil. He had raised us since birth, and taught us how to look after the world. An even greater problem though, was that he left behind his sovereign powers. My grandfather was one of the four sovereigns, the sovereign of water. So, now we had his powerful sovereign powers left behind. If anyone claimed them, they would take his place as the water sovereign. At my grandfather's funeral, my father appeared. He tried to make us tell him where we had put Poseidon's powers. We wouldn't tell him. He wanted to steal them, use them, gain ultimate power so he could rule the world single-handed with his army of fiends. So, my sisters and I now had a dilemma. What were we going to do with our grandfather's possessions? The mythical animals of the world went out of order. There needed to be four strong characters to keep them in line, but with one gone they went into a conflict with the world and each other. In the end, we developed a kind of box. We created the five keys. We managed to encase all mythical animals that weren't Gods or high in some way into the box. When all the animals were in, we used the five keys to seal the box. Until now, I didn't think the box could be re-opened without the keys. We must have made a mistake. We then locked our grandfather's possessions away into a secret room, which could only be found by whoever held the five keys. So we went into hiding, hoping that no one would find us." All went quite after the Sphinx finished speaking, apart from the birdcalls high up in tree. After a few seconds, Katie-Anne got up the courage to speak again.

"But, I've studied Manticores. All they are, are giant lions with scorpion tails and wings, and not much stronger than a Chimera. So I don't understand how one

Manticore-"

"-You've found this place, so you have the right to know," interrupted the Sphinx. "It all starts with my mother, Irirus. Irirus was a goddess, more beautiful and powerful than you can imagine. She gracefully guarded this planet long before humans inhabited it. At that time, she did not know that this planet would be her downfall. She was forbidden by her father, our grandfather, to enter the mortal boundaries of Earth under any circumstances. One day, my mother betrayed my grandfather and went down to Earth. There, a Manticore saw her. He transformed himself into something Irirus would love, using powers of which we don't speak. They soon fell in love. We were soon born, but we were not as they expected. We were lion type creatures. My father ran away and broke my mother's heart. During their time together, Irirus had taught him a lot about the powers she had and the powers all the Gods and sovereigns had. Of course, our father devoted himself into claiming ultimate power, so he studied them. He soon became stronger than all other Manticores because he managed to grab his hands on a minor amount of power." Yet again, silence followed.

"Well everyone says you learn something everyday, but I didn't expect to learn something like this," replied Adam.

"I am most displeased to hear that my father is out in the world again, but there is no point crying over spilled milk. Ok, you know about the riddles of the Sphinx, don't you?"

"Yes, your sister told us," replied Katie-Anne.

"I will let you hear mine. If you can get the five keys before my father, there may still be hope yet. Ready? Here we go. This creature is intelligent and powerful, although it may go through many stages. Tell me, what creature walks on four legs in the morning, two legs at noon, and three legs in the afternoon?" asked the Sphinx, looking from Adam to Katie-Anne. Both of them seemed to be in deep thought.

"What do you think it is?" Katie-Anne asked.

"I don't know. I mean, what animal walks on three legs?"

"Yeah that is a tricky clue. Hmmm. WAIT- Adam I think I solved it. What if the parts of the day don't refer to the day itself, but a life cycle? Morning would be childhood, noon would be adulthood, and afternoon would be old age!" Adam thought about this for a moment.

"I still can't think of what it could be."

"Adam, it's a human!"

"Correct!" boomed the Sphinx.

"How in the world did you know that? I mean, since when has a human ever had three legs?"

"Well, at childhood, we walk on all fours when we crawl. Then, when we get older into adulthood we walk on two legs. This is the tricky part, when we get to old age we still walk on two legs, but some old age people need help walking, and they use a walking stick which counts as a third leg!" she said ecstatically.

"You are a very smart girl. No one has ever solved that riddle before, you should be very proud of yourself," said the Sphinx, beaming at Katie-Anne. Adam looked puzzled.

"I think from now on, I'll let you solve the riddles," he said, looking at her confused. "Well, so we get the key then?"

"Of course. I am going to miss it dearly. Kashka! Come!" the Sphinx shouted into the enormous unknown tree that grew high into the heavens. There was a loud screech from the top of the tree and a silhouette of a bird appeared from right at the top of the tree. Katie-Anne knew the bird must be big because the tree was very high up and the silhouette of the bird was about the size of a normal crow. The bird silhouette darted down. Every second it got bigger and bigger until Katie-Anne got convinced it wasn't a bird that was zooming towards them. She was wrong. Eventually it did arrive. The bird was an enormous falcon, about the size of a fairly large mansion. The falcon was beautiful. The falcon bore majestic bronze and red plumage that was smoothed over by a lovely down. The falcon had three elegant silver feathers sprouting from the tip of its forehead. Its golden beak was long and curved at the end. The falcon's powerful talons were also bronze in colour and each about the size of an average sized shed. Attached to one of its legs via a rope was a bronze box encrusted with small emeralds that gleamed slightly.

Katie-Anne and Adam just looked at the falcon in awe. Neither of them had ever seen anything so beautiful and so powerful.

"This is Kashka. He is a species of falcon called 'Falcbasilicus', meaning 'Royal Falcon'. He is almost the last of his kind. They are the most loyal animals of the planet. They will help you whenever you need it. This is the first time I've seen my good old friend again since he was put into the Golden Box. Even though he did no wrong to the world, all mythical animals had to be locked up unfortunately," the Sphinx told, admiring her old friend. Katie-Anne looked sadly upon Kashka, knowing that if they were successful in their mission, Kashka would be locked away again.

The Sphinx moved towards Kashka and cut away the rope with her paw from the bronze box. The Sphinx picked it up with her scorpion tail and dropped it in front of Katie-Anne and Adam.

"The key is in there," she said, looking sadly towards the box, knowing that she had to let go. Katie-Anne and Adam didn't say or do anything. "Well, open it then, it's yours now." They moved towards the box. Adam tried to lift it up, but it was much too heavy. Instead, both of them crouched down. There was a strange lock on the front of the box. As Katie-Anne reached for it, the lock clicked open. Katie-Anne nervously grabbed the latch of the lock and pulled the lid open. A mass of bright green light rose from inside the box. Something small and round rose from the light and into the air. It stayed afloat above the box. The box flung itself shut and the round object dropped onto the lid. Katie-Anne and Adam starred at it. It was a small green orb about the size of a tennis ball. Katie-Anne picked it up to look at it. She noticed that there seemed to be a strange green misty texture, like clouds inside the orb, moving rapidly.

"That's the key? It looks nothing like a key!" Adam hissed quietly.

"A key is not necessarily a funny 3D metal object you stick inside a lock or hole. Keys come in many forms, some very secretive or maybe, not even physical," said the Sphinx, smiling gracefully. "I ask you one thing now that you have the key. You must promise me on this or you must understand I cannot let you leave. You must not use that key for the wrong purposes. You must use it solely to try and get to Poseidon's possessions before the Manticore does. You will do your very best not to let it fall into the wrong hands. Do you promise me?" said the Sphinx, a very serious expression appearing on her face. Katie-Anne and Adam both looked her directly in the eye.

"Of course I promise. I won't let you down," replied Katie-Anne.

"Ditto that," said Adam.

"In that case, you need to go and locate another key. I would advise going to the Alps. Another of my sisters lives there."

"How're we meant to get to the Alps?" Adam asked pompously.

"Kashka will fly you to the Alps happily." Kashka called in agreement. "If you ever need help for anything on this quest, call Kashka and he will fly to your immediate aid. He understands that this is very important and is willing to do whatever it takes to help."

"And how is he going to hear us when we call, especially since he will be here and we will probably be on the other side of the world," Adam asked, trying to catch the Sphinx out. The Sphinx smiled.

"He will hear you. You have very little faith, and it is that lack of faith, if anything that will be your downfall on this quest." Adam fell silent immediately and flushed. "Well, for now this is goodbye. I hope we will see each other again soon before this is over." Kashka bent down as low as he could so that Katie-Anne and Adam could climb on. After about ten minutes of struggle, which resulted in poor Kashka having a lot of feathers pulled out, Katie-Anne and Adam were securely on.

"Kashka, away!" ordered the Sphinx. The Falcbasilicus spread its titanic wings and shot into the air like missile. The ride was surprising comfortable, despite the speed Kashka was going. There seemed to be some sort of aura around Kashka that prevented the wind whistling around Katie-Anne and Adam. The soft plumage of Kashka was soft and relaxing under Katie-Anne and Adam.

"I guess we are dealing with the Mountain Sphinx next then," said Adam as the Alps came into view. Slowly, Kashka began increasing latitude and scaled up the side of the Alps. Katie-Anne and Adam were absolutely freezing. They could both see ski-shops and Cable-Carts dotted around the mountain. Eventually they became so high up that there was no human life. Katie-Anne was positively freezing. She could never remember feeling so cold.

Eventually, when Kashka was satisfied with the height, he stopped and dropped Katie-Anne and Adam off. With a final squawk, Kashka took off.

"Kashka, wait!" Katie-Anne called desperately, shivering in the cold. " How do we get back down?" Kashka didn't turn or even look as if he was listening to what Katie-Anne was saying and just kept on flying.

"I thought you're meant to help us if we needed it!" Adam shouted angrily. Kashka disappeared into the clouds and was gone. "Where do we go from here?" he asked Katie-Anne, rapping his arms around himself desperately trying to warm up. They both looked around the mountain in all the directions, but neither direction seemed too appealing.

"We probably have to go up," said Katie-Anne, looking up the mountain, her teeth chattering uncontrollably.

"You suggest we climb this thing with no climbing equipment? I feel as if I'm going to die up here," replied Adam, starting to get a bit agitated.

"Oh stop being so melodramatic all the time! Kashka wouldn't have dropped us off here if he didn't think we'd be able to cope or get anywhere!" Katie-Anne retorted angrily.

"Oh, so you think I'm melodramatic now!?" Adam roared. The mountain shook a little as his voice echoed around it and a dollop of snow fell from above.

"We have to be quiet, we'll end up causing an avalanche," Katie-Anne whispered, yet again looking above her. Adam stared at her grumpily. "We need to find a way of going up," said Katie-Anne, still looking up into the mountain. "Adam, just go round there and see if you can find an easy passage going up."

"I'm not going anywhere!" replied Adam indignantly. "Why don't you go round there?"

"You're the man, you're meant to be strong and brave, so hop to it!"

"Who died and made you queen!?" Adam yelled, causing the mountain to shake again. "Anyway, what's all this stereotypical talk? 'You're the man you're meant to be strong and brave', you can easily go! You have the power of earth as well!" So their argument carried on. Both of their voices were rising and they were totally oblivious to the racket they were creating. Snow kept falling from above due to the vibrations. Their voices were so loud a small slide of snow crashed just in front of them, showering them in snow. Inside the snow that had fallen, were two weird beasts never seen by either of them before. They looked roughly like large gorillas, except these animals were covered in light, greyish fur. They each had foot long nails on their hands and feet. Their eyes were blue and wide and looked like alien eyes. Katie-Anne ceased talking at once. They faced the beasts, terrified.

"Katie-Anne, what are they?" Adam asked, looking at the beasts.

"If I didn't know better, I'd say they are Yetis," whispered Katie-Anne trying not to move her lips too much.

"Yetis!" Adam yelled.

"Adam, be quiet! Stay absolutely still; they are like bears, just stand perfectly still" she hissed in return. The Yetis roared and began beating their chests. "I think they're a little upset with us for making them fall." The Yetis charged. Thinking fast, Katie-Anne whipped her hand to her side and the rose whip appeared. Katie-Anne drew the whip back proudly and whipped it at the Yetis. The first Yeti was caught around the legs. It lost its balance and fell onto the snow with a loud 'thump'. The second Yeti caught the whip in his hand and yanked it. Katie-Anne was pulled through the air and landed on the snow. Adam thought about the Planetary Sand and unleashed its power against the standing Yeti. The different coloured sand erupted from the palm of his hand and attacked the Yetis face. The Yeti stamped around, temporarily blinded. The Yeti that had fallen to the floor got up and relinquished what appeared to be some sort of black ice upon Adam. The ice was very sticky and it bound Adam's hands to his sides and his feet to the floor. Before Katie-Anne could get back up, one of the Yetis picked her up in his hand and lifted her into the air. He began to tighten his grip. Katie-Anne gasped in pain and desperately tried to pull herself away from the crushing grip.

Just as she gave up, she heard the beating of enormous wings above her. At first she thought Kashka had returned to help them, but when she looked up she saw a dark purple dragon come soaring down upon the Yeti that bound her. Katie-Anne had never studied a dragon that had looked like this before. It was spectacular. It was about the size of fern tree. Its whole body was dark purple in colour. It had two strange translucent purple-blue horns protruding from the top of his head. The claws on his hands and feet were also made of this strange texture. The tip of its tail ended in a small purple orb, which also looked like it was made out of the same thing as its horns and claws. Its vast wings were also purple in colour, but were lighter than its body, and were more like the colour of his eyes, which were lavender.

The purple dragon came soaring down and knocked the Yeti over. It relinquished its grip on Katie-Anne and she fell to the floor, feeling winded. Both Yetis glowered angrily at the dragon. The purple dragon bared its teeth at the Yetis. Katie-Anne and Adam noticed that its teeth also seemed to be made of the same material as the dragon's claws and horns.

The dragon roared and sent a jet of violet fire into the air. The Yetis growled angrily and fled back up the mountain. Katie-Anne was still gasping on the snow and Adam was still encaged in the sticky black ice. The dragon flew down and landed in front of them.

"Are you alright?" it asked in a very bark like growl.

"Um, yes thanks," Adam replied in a very small voice.

"Um, what exactly are you…I mean, who are you?" asked Katie-Anne. The dragon laughed in the same barky tone.

"My name is Drakite, and I am a species of dragon known as the Tragonzite," replied the dragon.

"We've never heard of a Tragonzite before," replied Katie-Anne.

"Tragonzites are dragons that possess tanzanite formations. My entire skeletal structure is made of tanzanite, so that's why my teeth, horns and claws are as well. Unfortunately, there are only about five or six Tragonzites left. In the time we roamed this planet, the intelligent creatures hunted us for the tanzanite qualities we have."

"That's awful," replied Katie-Anne sympathetically. "We were just wondering, how come you came to our aid?"

"I saw the Falcbasilicus drop you off, so I guessed from where you must have come."

"And where would that be?" Adam asked suspiciously.

"The Forest Shrine of course. The home to the Forest Sphinx."

"But, how do you know the whereabouts of the Sphinx!" asked Katie-Anne in shock.

"I am a great protector of the Sphinxes. I knew you must have come from the Forest Shrine because I heard you all that Falcbasilicus 'Kashka', and I know that a Falcbasilicus called Kashka lives with the Forest Sphinx."

"But that still doesn't explain why you wanted to help us," said Adam impatiently.

"I rescued you because I know the mission you have both been burdened with. I know that the Manticore is after the great water sovereign's power, and I want to help prevent that. My species was an ancient kind, with a kind and loyal heart. We have always helped those that need us most."

"Well, if you want to help us, that's fine by us. The more help we get the better. Let me introduce us to you. My name is Katie-Anne, and this is my colleague Adam."

"Very nice to meet you both," replied Drakite, bowing them.

"No matter how I like this little chat, WILL someone please release me from this stupid ice!" he said loudly.

"Oh sorry Adam I forgot. I don't know what I can do to get you out," said Katie-Anne apologetically, looking around the black ice.

"Let me help. This wont hurt you a bit Adam, so don't cower," Drakite said calmly.

"Why, what are you going to-" but before Adam finished speaking, Drakite let out a burst of purple fire straight at Adam. Adam was petrified. The flame struck and licked around him. But, Adam didn't feel a thing. The flame was curling around him melting away the black ice, but it didn't affect him in the slightest. In mere moments, the black ice had melted away and Drakite stopped.

"How, how'd you do that?" asked Adam, still trying to get round his head what had happened.

"Tragonzites were given the gift to be able to use a special fire rather than ordinary fire. This fire is special in that we can decide when to extinguish the fire we produce, and we can also decide what it harms. In this case, I decided that I wanted to affect the ice around you but not to affect you in the slightest," explained Drakite.

"That's a very powerful and useful tool," replied Katie-Anne.

"Yes it is. But first, what brings you here? Do you want to find the Mountain Sphinx?" asked Drakite, changing the subject.

"Just a second. How'd you know we were on a mission in the first place? It's fair enough if you guessed we came from the Forest Shrine, but how'd you know we are trying to get to Poseidon's power?" Adam asked suspiciously.

"A few days ago, I was approached by a young man. He told me the quest you were on and asked me to help you. He showed me pictures of you so that I would recognise you."

"A man asked you to follow us?" Katie-Anne whispered is shock.

"What man!?" Adam spat angrily, "are we being followed?"

"Adam, I just had a thought. I wonder if this has anything to do with our Mystery Man. We haven't heard from him for a long time," Katie-Anne said thoughtfully.

"Good thinking, it must be, we don't know of anyone else following us, do we?" replied Adam, calming down and also going into thought.

"Drakite, could you give us a description of what this man looks like please," Katie-Anne asked.

"Let me think. I remember, he had a slightly tanned skin; his hair was tied in dreadlocks and was dark in colour. I think he had a small goatee…and that's all I can remember, sorry," replied Drakite. Katie-Anne submerged herself yet again into thought. Who could be following them?

"We can't worry about that now. Drakite, do you know how far we have to travel to get to the Mountain Sphinx?" Adam asked hopefully.

"Yes, I do. I know the whereabouts of all the Sphinxes. The Mountain Sphinx is about a further mile up this mountain," Drakite replied confidently.

"Can you take us there now?" Adam asked hopefully. Drakite shook his head gently.

"No, I cannot take you there now, it is far too late in the day and it will be too dangerous. At night, a lot of dangerous creatures come out on this mountain and I can't risk anything happening to you. I will take you there tomorrow morning. If we leave early enough, we may avoid the Kobolticles."

"What are Kobolticles?" Adam asked curiously. Drakite sniggered to himself.

"They are quite stupid really, but are very dangerous in groups. Do you know what a Kobold is?" Drakite asked. Adam shook his head in puzzlement but Katie-Anne replied at once.

"A Kobold is a small dwarfish type creature that clean very old houses. Some Kobolds are wicked and lead you into death so they can steal your food," Katie-Anne gabbled.

"Yes, that's right. Well, Kobolticles are another type of Kobold, except they are made out of ice. They also have different legs to other Kobolds and they resemble frog's legs. They do a lot of jumping and bouncing to hunt and to live. Kobolticles are vicious. Whenever you enter one of their nests they will attack you immediately with no mercy. Thankfully, they are not very bright," replied Drakite. "They camouflage exceptional well so I want to avoid them if I can."

"Cant we take a route where there are little or no Kobolticles?" asked Katie-Anne.

"It wouldn't help even if we could. The Sphinx lives in a cave that furrows deep into the mountain, and a cave like this is like a haven for Kobalticles." Katie-Anne bowed her head in disappointment. "I think it would be wise if you camp here tonight."

"Camp here! We'll freeze before we set up camp!" Adam protested. Drakite smiled.

"You won't freeze." Drakite opened his mouth and coughed. A ball of his purple fire boomed from his mouth and struck the ground. Even though there was no wood or grass to set fire to, the flame stayed alight. It melted all the snow in a meter radius of it. The fire grew to the size of a small bonfire.

"As long as you stay near that fire, you will be warm, and nothing will touch you."

"Why wouldn't anything touch us?" asked Katie-Anne.

"Trangonzites are very powerful dragons. We are the strongest creatures this high up on the mountain, and a ball of purple fire is a warning to all others to keep well away if they wish to live."

"Won't the fire burn out eventually, I mean, nothing is even keeping it alight," Adam asked looking curiously at the fire.

"The fire will only die down when I want it to, and never before. I need to go, I have things to be doing before I retire for the day."

"You're not staying!? I know we will be safe, but what if something tries to attack us anyway?" Adam said desperately.

"I need to. Stop worrying you shall not be harmed. I will be back to pick you up in the morning." With that, Drakite expanded his titanic wings and took off into the sky and vanished.

"So, Drakite is quite cool, don't you think?" Adam asked sounding impressed.

"Yeah, he is. I'm glad we've got someone like him on our side," replied Katie-Anne, thinking about something that was troubling her.

"Well, you don't seem to enthusiastic about him. I would of thought you would be very interested in Drakite, him being mythical and all," said Adam, looking into Katie-Anne's face. "What's wrong?"

"I just want to know who's following us. The folder on my desk, the phone-call, the writing on the bus and the writing in my room. Do you think it's the same person?" asked Katie-Anne looking hopefully at Adam.

"Well, I presume so," replied Adam slightly taken aback by this sudden thought. "We can worry about this when we need to. Lets just set up camp now before its gets too dark."

*

It didn't take long for Katie-Anne and Adam to erect the single shabby tent. They crawled inside and curled up in their sleeping bags. The flashing of the purple flame was flickering from the entrance of the tent and was very warm. They slept completely untroubled, and true to Drakite's word, nothing tried to attack them.

When dawn approached, Katie-Anne and Adam heard the beating of huge wings. Their tent fluttered as though it was caught in a high wind. The tent was then ripped off the ground, and Katie-Anne and Adam looked up suddenly, their eyes narrowed against the sunshine. Drakite was standing above them holding the tent. Drakite glanced over at his fire, and it died down at once.

"Come on, time to go," he growled.

"Why do we have to go so early?" Adam complained, and yawning loudly.

"I explained it to you. We need to avoid the Kobalticles. And all the other monsters that may pose a threat will still be asleep," Drakite replied.

Katie-Anne and Adam had a very quick breakfast of stale tinned soup before packing away their damaged tent and sleeping bags.

"Right, climb on my back," Drakite instructed.

"Umm, how exactly?" Adam asked, looking nervously at Drakite's back.

"Just jump on to my back without damaging my wings and Adam, you can cling on to my neck, and you Katie-Anne can cling on to Adam." It was very difficult. Adam got on all right, but Katie-Anne kept slipping down. In the end, she used her earthen powers to raise the ground she was standing on a few meters like a podium. She climbed on easily after that and clung on to Adam.

"Are you secure? Good, then we're off!" Drakite expanded his vast purple wings and took off. The ride wasn't nearly as bad as what Katie-Anne and Adam first expected. His scales were not very slippery and had a fairly good grip.

After they had flown so high, they saw a large opening in the mountain face. Long, sharp icicles were spearing down from the entrance roof. They glistened beautifully as the sunlight caught them. The interior of the cave was extremely dark and Katie-Anne thought to herself how they were going to navigate inside.

"Well, lets go in then," Drakite growled confidently. Katie-Anne and Adam slipped easily off his back and Drakite walked into the cave. Katie-Anne and Adam followed pursuit, not knowing what would await them.

Chapter 9
The Temple in the Sky

The cave was exceptionally dark and eerie. There was a gentle constant drip coming from above, which Katie-Anne guessed must be full of ice. Then suddenly, a bright, lavender light filled the room. Both Katie-Anne and Adam blinked furiously as their eyes adjusted. When they looked up, they saw Drakite looking at them from in front. The purple orb on his tail was emitting the lavender light like a light bulb.

"You didn't tell us you could do that with your tail," said Adam, half annoyed half impressed.

"Well, you didn't need to know about it until now," replied Drakite laughing a little.

"You're full of useful surprises aren't you?" said Katie-Anne, beaming. Now that their eyes were adjusted, Katie-Anne and Adam and Drakite could finally see what the passage looked like. The walls of the cave seemed to be frosted over with a thin layer of ice. The floor was hard and slippery as it was full of water. The roof of the cave was very high, and it was filled with very long and sharp icicles that looked as though they could break off at any time. It was these icicles that seemed to making the gentle dripping noise as they melted. Just before Katie-Anne averted her gaze, she saw something small and clear scuttle across an icicle. She blinked and looked again. Whatever it was had gone, and she thought she must be seeing things out of lack of sleep.

As they walked in further, it became increasingly cold. Katie-Anne and Adam shivered and pulled their jackets closer around themselves. Soon they were so deep that they couldn't tell one end from the tunnel to the other. Both ends were completely dark. The only light was coming from Drakite's tail.

"How much further is it?" Adam hissed, shivering uncontrollably.

"I don't know, I've never been here before. But just stay on your guard, there could be anything lurking in here," replied Drakite, with a slight tone of fear in his growl. Then from up above, they heard noises, like a cat scratching at a sofa. They all looked up. It was a good thing they did because about six sharp icicles had broken free from the ceiling and were about to fall right on top of them. Drakite let out a stream of fire that melted the icicles, dousing them all in water. Then another broke off and narrowly missed Katie-Anne, as it pierced the floor like a sword. All of them looked up again. Near the stumps of the ruined icicles were what seemed to be very small little men made of blue ice. They were clinging to the ceiling with sharp little ice claws protruding from their hands and feet. They had frog like legs and some of them bounced along the ceiling. They had fluffy white beards growing from their icy chins. Their wicked beetle black eyes were glowering at Katie-Anne and Adam and Drakite malevolently.

"Kobalticles!" Drakite growled viciously, glaring at the Kobalticles with distaste. The Kobalticles brandished their fists at the heroes below and sliced through more icicles with their sharp claws. The icicles were falling like bombs. Drakite swished his titanic illuminated tail round and smashed the icicles out of the way. Some exploded on impact, others were hit back towards the ceiling. The little Kobalticles squealed in fright and bounced away as they icicles made contact with the ceiling, showering them all in ice. All the Kobalticles went scurrying away, some squealing in terror, others in anger, shaking their tiny little fists at the heroes.

"Well that got rid of them!" Adam laughed. The trio continued onwards.

"They are very annoying, Kobalticles," Drakite growled as they kept on moving. "They may not look like much, but they can be fairly powerful in numbers. With mythical animals, you should never judge by what you see, and you shall learn that soon enough." Neither Katie-Anne nor Adam knew how to reply to this, so they both stayed silent.

Finally, in a matter of minutes they found the end of the tunnel. It was just a normal ice covered wall. However, on this wall was a large blue talisman representing a snowflake. On either side of the talisman, there were two metal brackets, both frozen in ice. However, both of them were sporting light blue flames that cast a beautiful glow on the talisman. Drakite examined the talisman and smiled.

"So, what do we have to do here?" Katie-Anne asked. Drakite didn't answer for a few moments.

"I have a theory. I think it must be…there can be no other way…so they did have…just wait here for a moment, I'll be back in a minute," Drakite replied, hurrying off back in the opposite direction. About ten seconds after Drakite left, they heard a roar in the distance and heard the breath of fire. There were more shrieks from Kobalticles, and then Drakite returned. He had a Kobalticle clamped tightly in his right hand. The Kobalticle was squealing and banging its tiny fists angrily on Drakite's closed fist.

"Why have you brought *that*?" Katie-Anne asked, looking at the Kobalticle in disgust.

"I don't think the door will open until the power of ice has been revealed upon it," replied Drakite moving back towards the talisman.

"Door?" Adam whispered and Katie-Anne shrugged.

"Use some of your ice powers on the wall!" Drakite growled viciously at the Kobalticle. It shook its head stubbornly.

"Do it!" growled Drakite; hurling smoke out of his nostrils, which covered the Kobalticle in soot. It coughed. The Kobalticle murmured angrily and sent a small cloud of snow towards the wall. The snow cloud gently glittered on the talisman. Then the talisman began to flash blue and its shape began to change. The talisman lengthened and formed into a rough iron door with a door handle made of ice. Drakite let go of the Kobalticle and it scuttled away, murmuring angrily to itself.

"This is it!" squeaked Katie-Anne excitedly. She grabbed the door handle and withdrew her hand at once as though it had been burned. "Its so cold!" Katie-Anne murmured as she cradled her shivering hand. Adam put his hand into his jumper and grabbed the doorknob. He could still feel the cold, but not as much now that he had protection. He turned the handle gently and flung the door open. The room inside was very small. It was lit with more torches that housed bright blue flames. A large iceberg stood in the centre of the room. A gentle white glow seemed to be coming from inside it. When the heroes walked into the room, they found it was very icy and slippery and they had to hold onto the walls to stop themselves from falling over.

They weren't in the room ten seconds when something pounced from the back wall and skidded gently on the ice, landing in front of them. When it came to a halt, they saw who it was at once.

"Who are you?" it asked gently.

"You are one of the Sphinx sisters, and we are here to try and gain your key so that we can stop a great evil from gripping this fragile world," Drakite replied plainly as though he thought the Sphinx didn't deserve to know.

"My key? Ah, I sense something about you two," replied the Sphinx happily, looking over at Katie-Anne and Adam. "You are obviously the ones that my sister the Desert Sphinx told me about." Katie-Anne and Adam gapped at each other. "Yes, she contacted me right after you left her statue. I have been expecting you." She suddenly turned to look at Drakite and put on a politely puzzled simper. "But, I haven't been expecting you. Who are you, a friend, or a tagalong?"

"Watch it!" Drakite growled.

"Drakite, no!" shouted Katie-Anne exasperatedly. "She's just winding you up." The Sphinx was looking at Drakite still with the same simper as though daring him to attack.

"Can we, just, get to the matter in hand?" asked Adam nervously as he looked between the feuding.

"Yes, yes of course. You shall hear my riddle, and you must solve it. You will be allowed three guesses. If all three guesses are incorrect, then you must leave and are free to try again in another five hundred years-"

"Five hundred years!" Adam yelled, looking shocked.

"Yes, five hundred years. I will only let you hear my riddle if you give me your word that the tagalong will not guide you or give you any assistance." She looked at Drakite again as though hoping he would react. He growled again and Katie-Anne swore she could see his lavender eyes turning red.

"Don't worry, I wont help them. With a brain like yours, I'm sure a two year old could solve this riddle." Drakite smiled triumphantly, but the Sphinx merely nodded her head as though impressed with his come back.

"So, are you both ready? Sure? Ok then here is my riddle. I will repeat it as many times as necessary. It is hard, so take your time on it:

With potent, flowery words speak I,
Of something common, vulgar, dry;
I weave webs of pedantic prose,
In effort to befuddle those,
Who think I wile time away,
In lofty things, above all day
The common kind that linger where
Monadic beings live and fare;
Practical I may not be,
But life, it seems, is full of me!

"Tell me, what am I describing?" Katie-Anne and Adam gazed at each other. Judging by the looks on each other's faces, neither of them had a clue. They gazed at Drakite but he was slumped against the wall looking grumpy.

"Could we have it again please?" Katie-Anne asked. The Sphinx repeated it.

"So you speak with strong words. Ok we'll have to come back to that," said Katie-Anne thoughtfully.

"I don't get the next line at all," replied Adam befuddled.

"*I leave webs of pedantic prose.* Hmm, I suppose that would be sort of a concern for speech or writing," said Katie-Anne ignoring Adam. "*In a effort to befuddle those.* So far, we've got that whatever the Sphinx is describing speaks in strong words, and expresses concern for speech or writing in order to confuse people. Then I suppose the next line means to waste time…"

"How can she solve through these things?" Adam whispered to himself as he watched Katie-Anne solve the riddle.

"…lofty things, above all day? I don't have a clue what that could mean…"

"Don't worry Adam, Katie-Anne will get it," Drakite growled from the corner. Meanwhile, Katie-Anne kept muttering to herself and reciting pieces of the riddle. Sometimes she wore a smile of triumph, as though she was very close to solving the riddle. At other times, she looked blatantly puzzled, and sometimes a little disappointed.

At last, after five painful minutes Katie-Anne clapped hands together and smiled.

"I think I've done it!" she squeaked excitedly. "I think it is one of two things. I just hope one of them is right." Drakite and Adam sighed with relief but it was not over yet. What if she was wrong?

"Mountain Sphinx, I have an answer." The Sphinx simpered at her politely.

"Well, let me hear your first guess."

"Is the answer, and author or writer?" Katie-Anne asked nervously, hoping she was right. The Sphinx's smile widened.

"Oh no, I am sorry to regret that the answer you have supplied is incorrect," Katie-Anne closed her eyes for a few seconds and when she opened them she looked as though she had not yet given her first answer. "You have two more guesses before you must leave this place." Drakite looked slightly anxious and sweat began trickling gently down Adam's face. Katie-Anne gulped and then answered again,

"My second guess is a riddle or a riddler." She closed her eyes, hoping beyond hope this was the right answer; it just had to be…

"I am glad to tell you that that is the correct answer." Katie-Anne opened her eyes and let out a gasp of relief. Adam whooped and Drakite took a deep relieving breath. The Sphinx was still simpering.

"Well done human girl, I did not expect you to solve that riddle so quickly. You have already shown that you have an exceptional aptitude for this quest." Katie-Anne blushed. "As promised, I will pass on the key that I have been guarding." The Sphinx raised a paw into the air and the iceberg in the middle of the room began to shake. Solid ice began crumbling from the tip. Eventually, a hole opened up near the tip and a strong silver light issued from it followed by a silver box frosted over in ice. The box travelled over to the Sphinx and landed on the slippery ice in front of her. Katie-Anne noticed that the latch was frosted over.

"You may proceed in taking the key, humans. However, I do not want the tagalong touching the box because he is so clumsy he'll probably leave great gashes in the silver." The Sphinx smiled tauntingly at Drakite again, who in turn flapped his wings furiously and issued a smoke ball from his nostrils.

"Drakite, just leave it!" Adam shouted quickly as Drakite showed a lot of interest in attacking the Sphinx. Katie-Anne crept towards the box and the ice around the latch immediately thawed. She gripped it and swung it open. As the lid opened, even more bright sliver light erupted from inside, giving the walls and ice a beautiful moonlit glow. A small object was just visible rising out of the box, before the lid snapped shut, the silver light vanished, and a small orb landed on top of the box. It was the key. It was identical to the key they had recovered from the Forest Sphinx, except that this key was silver in colour rather than green. Katie-Anne picked it up. It was very cool and about as heavy as the other key.

"I beg of you that you stop my father from reaching Poseidon's possessions first. You MUST stop him at all costs. If he ever got any sovereign power, I don't even want to think what irreversible trouble that would cause. Do not take him lightly, as you have no idea what he is capable of," the Sphinx told, no longer supporting a simper, but a grave resentful sadness.

"But what should we do with Poseidon's possessions once we find them? We can't hide them again, can we?" Katie-Anne asked curiously.

"No, we cannot hide them anywhere else. We must initiate a new water sovereign. The problem is, finding one," replied the Sphinx. She heaved a great sigh a beckoned them to leave. They bid farewell to the Sphinx and departed back into the ice cave. The door turned back into a wall with the talisman gleaming beautifully. Meanwhile, Drakite was looking furious.

"Drakite, why was that Sphinx being so horrible to you?" Adam asked nervously, glancing up at the murderous look upon Drakite's face.

"Well, I've told you before, I know all the Sphinx. I get on well with all the Sphinxes except this one. It's too much of a long story to tell. All you need to know is that we had a very big argument a long time ago and we ended up fighting. I was punished for fighting someone superior to me. I think the Sphinx was trying to entice me to fight her again." There was a short pause following this.

"But, doesn't she realise we are all on the same side?" Katie-Anne asked.

"The Sphinxes are good, yes. But they don't want to part with their keys. They know they have to give us the keys or risk letting the Manticore taking them but they still don't feel comfortable letting go. It's like, a mother having an only child. This child is about to start university. The mother doesn't want to part with her child yet, but she knows she must to give her child the best future possible. Do you understand now?"

"Yes, it's a lot simpler when you put it like that," replied Katie-Anne.

Their discussions led them right back to the entrance of the cave. They had a few spots of trouble with the Kobalticles but Drakite made quick work of them.

"It's still very early in the day, so we could try and get another key. But no matter what, we must not spend any more time on this mountain. It gets more dangerous as the mythical animals become more confident," said Drakite, as they walked out of the dark tunnel into the fresh beaming sunlight.

"What do you think Katie-Anne? Where should we go next?" Adam asked.

"Why are you asking me?" said Katie-Anne

"Because you know more about the Sphinx than I do and you are the one that has solved the riddles. If it wasn't for you, we'd be stuck at the statue still." Katie-Anne blushed furiously and tried not to look too modest.

"Well, I think it is up to Drakite to decide because he knows more about the Sphinxes than I do and he knows where to go next." They both looked at Drakite expectantly. Drakite looked taken aback that they wanted to go where he wanted to go.

"Well, I think may be the Temple of Nimbus would be our best bet," Drakite replied. "That's where the Sphinx bearing the wind key resides," he added looking at the puzzled expressions on their faces.

"Where is it?" Katie-Anne asked confidently, but she had a shrewd suspicion where.

"It is high in the sky, above the clouds," replied Drakite proving Katie-Anne right. "The Temple of Nimbus was created by the Zephyr Dynasty."

"Who were they?" Adam asked interestedly.

"They were once ordinary people of Earth, who lived when the mythical animals were still around. Somehow, but no one knows how, they evolved and developed the power to control the wind. There were seven, I think. Anyway, they were not well loved on Earth. They were treated with the same prejudice as witches were in medieval times. Anyway, because of this, they built a sanctuary, a kind of plateau, high in the sky where no one could reach them. They lived and bread until their population grew out of control. So they left the Temple of Nimbus and built a city in the sky. But unfortunately, I do not know where that is. They haven't been seen since they left the temple. When it was abandoned, the Sphinx that guarded the skies decided to take refuge there." Katie-Anne and Adam listened with awe, and were very impressed.

"Do you think they died out Drakite?" Katie-Anne asked.

"No, I don't think so. I think they are still out there, just undiscoverable." Drakite turned away and looked into the sky.

"But Drakite, if it is so high in the sky, we wont be able to breath properly because the air is too thin," said Adam, also beginning to look into the sky as though hoping he was about to spot the temple.

"The Zephyr Dynasty used their powers to secure an aura around the temple to have the same air pressure and density on the temple, and to let the cloud support its weight."

"That's gotta be some pretty nifty powers they had," Adam whispered to Katie-Anne who nodded in agreement.

"Right, well I better go and find the Temple of Nimbus," Drakite growled.

"But I thought you knew where it is!" Katie-Anne said anxiously.

"I don't know it's precise location. Listen, I'll take you back home and I'll come to pick you up when I've found it."

"What do you mean? Why can't we come with you?" replied Adam angrily.

"It'll be too risky. Finding the Temple requires going high above the clouds. There may not be enough air for you to breath!"

"What about you, wont you be able to breathe?" asked Katie-Anne.

"I am a dragon. I am designed to fly higher than where we are planning to go. I'll be able to breath don't you worry."

With no further arguments, Katie-Anne and Adam climbed onto Drakite's back and they took off.

"Drakite I was wondering. Could you tell us a bit about the sovereign? We've heard bits about them, but could you tell us the full story?" Adam asked inquisitively. Drakite considered him for a moment.

"Well, ok. I may end up repeating things you already know, but don't interrupt my story. There were four sovereigns. They each control an element: water, fire, earth and wind. These are the four foundations of the planet. They originated from a different galaxy. They began like everything else. Single-celled organisms. But when they grew, they were extremely powerful. They kept evolving and their powers deepened further. Eventually, they came to an agreement to start their own galaxy. Thus, they created the Milky Way. They chose one particular planet to live on and decided they would create further insignificant life forms. This is where mythical animals come in. Other animals, everything from a whale, to a daphnia developed on their own accord. Now, the water sovereign was a giant merman named Poseidon. He had a beautiful daughter called Irirus. He forbade Irirus to enter Earth, as all four sovereigns lived in another dimension, which they also created. However, when Poseidon was not watching his daughter, she slipped away and went to Earth. There, she fell for a Manticore that took on the appearance of someone she would love. When Poseidon found out, he was furious. He was even more furious when he found out Irirus was expecting a baby. However, Irirus gave birth to five babies, not one. They were the Sphinxes. Irirus died at childbirth. Poseidon was the weakest of the sovereign and already had enough scandals in his life. He was on the brink of death himself.

He spent the remaining of his years raising his five granddaughters. They were to enter Earth one day and guard it. But by this time, natural progression meant that by now, people inhabited the Earth. Poseidon absolutely forbade the Sphinxes being seen by intelligent eyes. However, as I'm sure the Desert Sphinx told you, she was seen one day when she was trapped in a sandstorm. She had failed.

As I explained before, Poseidon was too old and weak to cope with any more scandals, and he died soon after. The world was left in a predicament. The mythical animals only lived in harmony as long as the four sovereigns were sill strong. This balance was lost, and the three remaining sovereigns left it up to the Sphinx to decide what to do. In the end, they decided to seal away all mythical animals that were not part of the sovereign's inner circle. The peace was restored. They had to prevent anyone from gaining Poseidon's sovereign power. All four sovereigns imbedded their powers in their personal items. So, the Sphinx took all of

Poseidon's items and hid them. They created five keys so that they could only be accessed when all keys are together.

However, there was another predicament that needed to be solved. The balance of the elements was fixed, but the balance of good and evil was not. In the end, the wind sovereign created something known as the 'Tao' or the 'Ying and Yang'. This balance could be controlled through this Tao. In the end, the wind sovereign came to be known as the 'Tao Master'." Drakite didn't pause once through his story and Katie-Anne and Adam clung onto every word.

"Who are the other two sovereign then?" Adam asked, curiosity swelling inside him.

"Well, the fire sovereign is a dragon. In fact, she is the Queen of Dragons. Her name is Tiamat. But she is not all too good. She keeps well away from the others. The earth sovereign is, you'll like this, Mother Nature." Katie-Anne gasped. "Hopefully, if everything goes to plan, you'll never need to meet any of the sovereigns."

"I'd love to meet a sovereign!" Katie-Anne sighed.

*

Drakite's story telling, and the discussions that continued after led them right back into England.

"We live in London Drakite."

"Ok, I'll take you there." Drakite made a smooth landing. "I don't know how long I will be, so don't wait for me. I'll get back as soon as I can." With that, he opened his wings and took back off into the sky, with people all around them gaping and looking up at him as he swerved in the sky.

"Do you have any money for a taxi?" Adam asked.

"It's just lucky I do," replied Katie-Anne, and she fished in her bag for her change. They caught the taxi, and they stayed at Katie-Anne's house. Katie-Anne felt good to be home. She ached all over because of the fight with the Stone Knight and the Yetis, the journey through the ice cave, and sleeping roughly on the mountain.

"At least we can get a decent night's sleep tonight," said Adam as he sat down on a sofa and began to watch television.

After about two hours, Adam decided he wanted a walk.

"Do you want to come too?" he asked Katie-Anne.

"Hang on then, I just need to close the windows." They left the house and set off at a brisk walk down the street. They passed a few people they knew.

"What are we going to do about Firebell?" Adam asked suddenly. Katie-Anne had forgotten completely about her job, and thought by now they would probably be sacked for not turning up to work.

"Well, we have more important things to worry about now. Losing a job doesn't mean anything compared to losing Poseidon's power."

"Very true." They both kept on walking. They took a short cut down a deserted dark alleyway fearlessly knowing that if anything tried to attack them, they had their powers at the ready. They noticed a man also walking down the alleyway, but coming towards them. As he passed them, Katie-Anne glanced at him and stopped still. She recognised his tanned skin, long dreadlock hair and his small goatee on his chin. Something clicked in her head.

"Hey! Wait a minute!" she shouted. The mysterious man sprinted away. Katie-Anne gave chase. Adam looked puzzled and followed.

"Katie-Anne! What are you doing!!?" he bellowed. Katie-Anne continued to run. She would not let the man out of her sight. She flung her palm forwards and a large lily vine burst from her hand and bound itself tightly around the man. He fell.

"So!" she said triumphantly, "you have been following us! Why!?" Adam caught up gasping for breath.

"Kate, what-?"

"The cleaner at the office, the gas attendant, the steward on the airplane. They were all you. I knew I recognised you! Adam thought I was mad. I kept telling him that I had been seeing you all over the place. Now, tell us why you have been following us!"

"I'm saying nothing, you crazy woman!" bellowed the trapped man. Katie-Anne raised her palm directly above the man's head.

"Spill it, or you'll be watering buttercups on your head for the rest of your life!" The man looked fearful for a moment.

"Ok! Ok, I'll tell you everything. I have been following you. I was the one who left the folder on your desk, I. was the one who told the Tragonzite to help you!" he bellowed angrily.

"But why? Who are you, anyway?" asked Adam, disgust etched into every part of his face.

"My name is Solomon. I have known about the powers and the legend of the Sphinxes for millions of years-"

"Millions of years!? But, surely you can't be human then?" asked Adam, now sounding totally shocked.

"Of course I'm not human! I am the uncle of the five Sphinxes. I am an immortal. The Sphinx's mother, Irirus, was my sister. I have been keeping an eye on the Sphinxes since I am their last living relative. Not that long ago, I found out that the Manticore had somehow prevented itself from being encased in the Golden Box. It had been weak for thousands of years because he had a terrible price to pay for tricking an immortal (Irirus). It is only now he has got his strength back. He wants revenge on the three sovereigns for making him live a life of curse for thousands of years. This is why he wants Poseidon's power.

I needed someone to get to the five keys before he did. If we could thwart him early, then he might not pose too much of a threat. But before he was stripped of his power, he gained a lot of power himself because of the information my sister disclosed to him. Now his years of punishment are over, he has regained all his old power.

I could have easily been the one to get the five keys before he did. But unfortunately, immortals are not allowed. So I had to find a clever-enough mortal who could. It was just my luck I heard about you. I took on a human form and decided to find as much about you as I could. I learned mythical animals fascinated you and your expertise on the subject were advanced. So I placed the folder on your desk. I went into the statue of the Sphinx myself and took photos of the tablet, much to my niece's displeasure. I placed all the information of the Sphinx you would need on your desk. I knew you would take up the task because I knew you were keen to prove yourself to your colleagues. So you went to the Sphinx and learnt the mythical animals were real. However, in doing so you did something that complicated matters. You unleashed all the mythical animals. But this turned out not to be such a bad thing. You gained the power to control earth. I knew this would be essential in combating the Manticore when the time came.

After I saw you enter the Amazon Rainforest, I immediately went to find the loyalist mythical animal I could find. I was lucky I found a Tragonzite. I told the Tragonzite the situation and he immediately took the post. He waited for you at the Alps, knowing you would need to find the Mountain Sphinx. And by all this, I merely hoped that you would become powerful enough to stop the five keys from falling into the wrong hands and destroy the Manticore forever." Katie-Anne and Adam stood dumfounded. They were completely shocked.

"But, why didn't you reveal yourself to use. Things could have gone a lot faster," said Katie-Anne.

"If you knew I could help you a lot, you would start to become lax and you wouldn't have put your full efforts in. I needed you to do it alone so you could grow strong enough," replied Solomon.

"Well, now that we know about you, will you help us now?" asked Katie-Anne hopefully. Solomon sighed.

"Yes I will. But just because I'm helping you, doesn't mean you cant put your full efforts in still. You must both understand. You must become as powerful as possible. Your earth powers are already growing remarkably. This lily vine is very powerful I am impressed. Just call upon me whenever you need me and I will help you." He closed his eyes and disappeared in a cloud of blue smoke, leaving the lily vine on the ground.

"Wow!" said Adam, still staring at the ground where Solomon had disappeared.

"That certainly explains a lot. But he never told us who left all those messages on the bus and the walls."

"May be he doesn't know."

"May be. And Adam," her voice suddenly became very stern, "you convinced me that me seeing this bloke all over the place was all in my head!! Somehow, 'I told you so!' doesn't quite satisfy me!"

"Ok I'm sorry, I made a bad mistake and it will never happen again. But like you said, I wish he could have told us who was giving us all those warnings."

*

A few days went by, but they heard no news from Drakite or Solomon. However, both Katie-Anne and Adam were now some sort of superheroes. It all started when Katie-Anne went into London to do some shopping. Some mythical animals began attacking Trafalgar Square, and she used her powers to drive them away. Now, they were both getting calls to help with monster situations, and television networks and newspaper journalists knocking on their doors day and night for interviews.

"Well, I always wanted to be famous," said Adam as he looked through the curtains of Katie-Anne's house to see the hundreds of people wanting interviews.

"It's not funny! They will never let us have peace!"

Katie-Anne's mind kept flickering to the idea of the Temple of Nimbus, and whether Drakite had discovered it yet. Most of the time she thought he couldn't have found it because he would surely come back and take them to it. But, no sooner was she thinking about this for the umpteenth time; Drakite came circling above them when they were sitting in the garden. He looked a little worse-for-wear. His beautiful purple scales had numerous bruises and burns. His wings had slight tears in them, and he held one at a slight angle. His nose was bloody and sore.

"Drakite!" Katie-Anne whimpered sympathetically, rushing over to Drakite and examining his injuries. Adam ran over too, looking half repulsed and half puzzled at the injuries.

"What happened to you!?" Adam demanded.

"Well, it looks like the Manticore has finally managed to gather some follows," replied Drakite, wincing as Katie-Anne dabbed his wounds with a cloth and some iodine.

"Followers?" Adam replied.

"Yes. When the creatures first came out of the Golden Box, they only did what they wanted to do. They listened to nobody. Now, some of them are on the side of the Manticore, working for him."

"But, how?" asked Katie-Anne.

"A variety of things. Persuasions, delayed promises, blackmail. Some of them are his natural allies and friends anyway." He broke off, looking quite worried.

"Is that how you sustained these injuries? Did they attack you?" Katie-Anne asked angrily.

"Yes. The Manticore is making his army to fight the good side. He places spies everywhere to look where the important men on our side are going; or take them out if they can." Katie-Anne looked horrified. Adam looked appalled.

"What are we going to do?" asked Katie-Anne.

"Do you remember me telling you about the Tao Master? You know, the wind sovereign and the guardian of the ying-yang?"

"Oh, yeah," replied Katie-Anne and Adam.

"The Tao Master is currently the only sovereign that is taking an active approach. At the moment he is the leader of the good army. So hopefully, we will soon have an army to combat the Manticores'."

"But why don't the fire and earth sovereign help?" Adam asked suspiciously.

"Tiamat, the fire sovereign, won't help because she has a dark nature and is very keen to see strife and struggle. She is neither good or bad, really, she likes to stay out of the way, or 'not to interfere' as she puts it. Mother Nature is the most powerful and the wisest of the sovereign. She can see the future with her husband, Father Time. They would love to help us, but they can't because it breaks their rules of not interfering with time."

"I don't understand," replied Katie-Anne.

"Think about it. If they can see the future, they are going to know what is going to happen in the war. If they tell us what is going to happen, we can change it, and change what we shouldn't. Father Time is a descendant of Time Clairvoyants, from another dimension. When he took control over time in this galaxy, he had to sign a pact saying he would not interfere with time unless it was strictly necessary. So the best thing we can do is hide both of them away as secure as possible so the Manticore doesn't get them." Katie-Anne's head was swimming. She couldn't believe that there were really people that controlled time and had the power to change it.

"So what do *we* do now?" asked Adam.

"Oh! Yes, sorry. I found the Temple of Nimbus. I would have got here yesterday but I had to resort to go through scenic routes and hidden valleys so that I wasn't beaten up."

"But you were anyway," Adam retorted, bitterly thinking of how much pain he was going to cause those for attacking Drakite.

"Well, yes. I came out to catch some food. There were five of them. Two Harpies, an Ogre, a Hameh, and finally, their leader, a Senmurv." Neither Katie-Anne nor Adam knew what a Senmurv was, but it sent a shiver down their spines.

"What's a Senmurv?" Katie-Anne asked.

"It is a vile, twisted, evil creature. Perfect, as he is one of the Manticore's captains. Basically, it is half mammal, half bird. It has the basic body of a gigantic peacock, the head of a savage dog, claws of a lion and wings of some evil bird." Both Katie-Anne and Adam shivered.

"How did you know it was working for the Manticore?" asked Adam.

"Simple. They all had bands around their arms or legs that had a symbol of the Manticore wearing a crown and killing the sovereign. Anyway, enough about the Manticore. Are you ready to go and get the third key?"

"But Drakite. You're hurt. Surely you're not up to flying again are you, especially with us on your back," Katie-Anne replied. Drakite snorted.

"Don't worry about it, I'm made of stronger stuff than you know. Just climb on and I'll take you there." Katie-Anne and Adam once again climbed onto Drakite's back with difficulty. Drakite winced every now and again when they touched or moved across his injuries.

Then they were off. Drakite keeping himself steady as they soared into the sky and left the ground far behind. They talked to Drakite the whole journey as they flew. They told him about the man they encountered in the alleyway, and he was very interested to hear about it.

Every now and again they would see a flying mythical animal coming in the other direction, or else overtake them. But then Katie-Anne became very worried as she thought what happened to Drakite on his other flight.

"Drakite? Are you sure we're safe? I mean, no one will attack us, will they?" Katie-Anne asked, hoping that she sounded off hand.

"No, it is highly unlikely we will be attacked because you two are with me. Usually, they try and pick us off one by one. They are too cowardly to have an honourable fight." Katie-Anne took a deep relieving breath. She felt a lot better now.

"Urm, Drakite? I was wondering. Because we, that is to say all humans, thought that mythical animals were never real," Katie-Anne glowered, "does that mean other things are real too? Like wizards, and the Lock-Ness Monster?" Drakite was silent for a few moments.

"Well, in theory, yes they do exist. But not in the way you think. The 'Lock-Ness Monster' is just an old made up hullabaloo. However there is some truth to it. There is a mythical animal that suits its description, however I have no idea what it is called, as I have never come across it.

As for wizards, only sorcerers exist. They deal in dark and dangerous powers. Magic in the way you believe, like waving a magic wand and saying a few silly words, does not exist. Sorcerers manipulate dark powers and fuse it with other powers, like elemental powers to create their own brand of evil powers."

"So, if sorcerers are bad then, does that mean the Manticore will have some on his army?" Katie-Anne asked seriously.

"I'm afraid it is a strong possibility, one which must not be ignored. Sorcerers are extremely powerful, and if you ever find your self coming across one, you must be fully prepared."

The trio continued talking through the whole journey. They talked mostly about the Manticore's army, and how to combat it. Then suddenly, Drakite began to slow down. He looked upwards into the highest clouds.

"You'd better hold on tight," he said to Katie-Anne and Adam. Then suddenly he rocketed upwards like a bullet. Eventually they burst through a clump of cumulonimbus clouds and into a clear patch of sky. Thundering through the clouds had soaked them all. But Drakite was still climbing higher, the air becoming increasingly cold and light. Adam and Katie-Anne began to feel the effects of the thin air. They felt extremely light headed, and tired, they could barely hold on. Then, as if an invisible force suddenly disabled Drakite, they had stopped. The air was normal again, and neither of them felt light headed anymore.

And there, gleaming and glistening in the sunlight in front of them, was a huge, towering temple, made of deep blue ice. The temple seemed to be supported on a sort of plateau that was in the shape of a bladder and made of white stone tinted with purple. Two lilac stone columns stood at either entrance of the temple. There were flowerbeds in the plateau floor, parallel to the columns and filled with flowers Katie-Anne had never seen before.

The roof of the temple itself was shaped like an upside-down bladder. On the very tip of the roof there was a small shining purple orb, similar to Drakite's tail. It was emitting a soft, purple light, like a beacon, which cast a beautiful glow on the plateau. In between the two columns, close to the flowerbeds, was a huge fountain that had statue of the Sphinx in the middle. It appeared to be made out of amethyst. Pure, clear water was poring out of the Sphinxes mouth, and the tip of the scorpion tail. The plateau itself was suspended on a dark grey, thick cloud.

The trio landed softly on the plateau.

"This is-remarkable," Adam murmured slowly, apparently lost for words. They slowly walked around the Sphinx Fountain, admiring the craft, and between the two columns, right up to the door, which was made of pink sapphire and the door handle encrusted with diamonds.

Katie-Anne gripped the handle tightly, and walked first into the room, finally about to see the old monument of the famous Zephyr Dynasty.

Chapter 10
The House of the Rising Tao

The room inside the temple was enormous, as well as tall. The walls were made of the same deep blue ice, and the ceiling was equivalent to the shape of the roof outside. However, right in the centre of the ceiling were small pink sapphires in a circle.

The centre of the room was taken up by another Sphinx fountain, very similar to the one outside, but bigger. There were numerous shelves and displays around the walls that held strange objects. Some were still, others were moving.

The far wall was taken up by four doors, each made of the same pink sapphire as the door that they had entered through, and each of the handles were encrusted with diamonds.

"I suppose we have to go through one of those doors. But which one?" Katie-Anne asked thoughtfully. Drakite walked towards the doors and picked up an old piece of parchment that was on the floor.

"Look at this! I think this tells us which door to go through," he growled. Katie-Anne hurried over. Adam was rather reluctant, as he wanted to look at the objects on the surrounding walls.

Drakite gave the piece of parchment to Katie-Anne, and she read it aloud:

One among our number will lead you to your doom
Another is just faking; and will lead you to no room.
A third is packed with monsters, for you to fight instead.
Another is the real thing, but do not lose your head!
At first glance the doors may all look the same,
But on the second from your right, the door is naught but lame!
The forth from not your left, is a danger to you all.

So it would be wise, to stay here in this hall!
The one left on the end, will lead you to no good.
The only thing that will be left of you will be the sour taste of blood!
Finally the door that remains will take you on your way.
Unless you're sure, don't take a door, if you wish to live past today!

All three of them just stared at the paper after Katie-Anne had finished reading.

"We're going to be stuck here for ever!" Adam spat angrily.

"Just be quiet for a minute!" Katie-Anne retorted. She read the parchment a few more times, and every time she looked up, she stared at each door, occasionally pointing at them, or else shaking her head. She read it one more time, looked up, and clapped her hands. "I've cracked it. Four doors. One is just faking, another is full of monsters, the other is full of danger, and one will take us to the Sphinx!"

"Do you know which one is which?" Drakite growled anxiously.

"I think so. The first door is full of monsters, the third door is fake, and the fourth one has unimaginable doom. That just leaves door number two."

"You're quite sure?"

"Almost certainly!" Katie-Anne walked towards the second door and gripped the handle. Adam was right behind her, and Drakite towered over them. Then, she forced the door open. Another large room awaited them inside. The walls were not made of blue ice, but of the same pink sapphires as the door. There was a huge purple stalactite dangling from the ceiling. What made this stalactite most unusual was that it had small circular holes all the way round it. The back wall was so dark that they couldn't see it; it was covered in shadow. Apart from that, the rest of the room was empty.

Then, as soon as Katie-Anne had put a foot through the door, hundreds of spikes ejected through the holes in the stalactite, but did not fire. Katie-Anne immediately thought they had entered the wrong door after all.

"Adam, look over my shoulder," she said nervously. Adam looked over and stared horrified at the spikes.

"We should go back," and he retreated immediately.

"No we shouldn't, it's a trick," Drakite replied at once. "Katie-Anne, Adam, walk into the room and get ready to defend yourselves." Katie-Anne took a few more steps. She then saw the spikes reach further out. She registered in about a split second that the spikes were about to fire at them. Katie-Anne pointed her hands forwards and an enormous tangled rhododendron plant erupted from them. At the same time, the spikes launched like missiles. All the spikes were engulfed by the rhododendron plant. When Katie-Anne was pretty sure they were safe, she let the plant fall to the floor in tatters.

"That was very close," whispered Adam.

"But I don't understand, if this is the right room, then that shouldn't have happened," Katie-Anne replied. As she spoke, bright purple light spilled from the holes in the stalactite. The light shaped itself and disappeared. The Sphinx was suddenly standing before them. She looked exactly like her sisters, except she was slightly purple in colour.

"As a matter of fact, the spike trap is here to sieve through all of those that come here. All those that are faint hearted would have run upon seeing the spikes. All the tough ones would have entered. And if they survived, I would have given them my key. And that, I presume, is why you are here?" said the Sphinx.

"Yes, we are. We know we have to solve a riddle that you tell us. So, could we hear yours please," replied Katie-Anne confidently.

"You've already solved it. The door riddle. And even if I did give you another to solve it would be pointless. I do not have to key anymore-"

"-Someone else has it?" Adam blurted.

"Yes, the Tao Master." There was a short pause.

"Well, that's ok then, because the Tao Master is the wind sovereign, he is on our side," Adam replied, almost laughing.

"Where is the Tao Master?" asked Drakite.

"I have no idea. The only one I know who knows, is the Tao Master himself. I do believe that after obtaining the key, he went and made himself harder to find so as to put a greater protection on the key."

"So, we can end this quest now then! If the Tao Master has one of the keys, there is no way we can be frightened of the Manticore getting Poseidon's powers!" Adam boomed happily. Drakite nodded happily, but Katie-Anne ignored them.

"Thank you for your time, Sky Sphinx, but we must be leaving," Katie-Anne said to the Sphinx.

"Wait a moment!" the Sphinx called. She opened her paw, and there sitting in her palm was a small round orb. At first, Katie-Anne thought it was the key, despite what they were told. Then she realised it couldn't be. The orb was a lot smaller. It also appeared to be some sort of eye. The orb was colourless, yet inside there was white mist. On the outside, there was a pattern, which looked like a cat's eye. "I'm sure you know what Elementites are. This is a wind Elementite. You probably can't control the power of wind yet but take it anyway. It's all I can offer you for solving the riddle and getting this far." Katie-Anne took the Elementite gently from the Sphinx.

"Thank you very much. We are trying to find as many Elementites as possible."

"It's a pleasure. I hope we shall meet again soon."

"So do we," replied Katie-Anne. They all bid farewell to the Sphinx and walked back into the main hall, and out into the open plateau.

"So, what are we going to do about the Tao Master?" Katie-Anne asked thoughtfully.

"Absolutely nothing," Drakite replied comfortably.

"Why not!?" replied Katie-Anne taken aback, and gazing at him suspiciously.

"Have you forgotten the real reason you both went on this quest to begin with? You set out to stop the Manticore from collecting the keys. If the Tao Master is in charge of one of those keys, there is no way the Manticore will find him, he is too heavily protected," Drakite replied matter-of-factly. Katie-Anne still looked at him, a slight twinge of anger on her face.

"I'm completely dumbfounded that you think this is the only reason me and Adam are doing this," she retorted. Adam looked slightly puzzled. "So, Drakite, Adam. You're both completely happy are you, that mythical animals are still roaming the planet, causing destruction left right and centre? We *need* the keys to reseal all of the mythical animals back into the Golden Box. Adam, how could you have forgotten what the Desert Sphinx told us so quickly? I don't care if either of you want to stop, but I'm going to continue and get those keys. It's my fault that the mythical animals have returned. If I hadn't been so stupid to have taken that expedition to the statue of the Sphinx, none of this would have happened!" She walked to the edge of the plateau and silently began to cry. Both Drakite and Adam looked ashamed of themselves.

"Katie-Anne, its not just your fault. Think about it. Remember the Manticore was never sealed in that box. He would still have gone after the keys. If we had never unleashed the monsters, we may have never heard about him and then it would have been to late to stop him!" Adam replied, trying to make her feel better. She turned around, tears clinging to her face. She rushed to Adam, gave him a swift kiss on the cheek, and hugged him tightly. He hugged her back. Drakite turned away awkward.

"The next thing, then, is to try and find the whereabouts of the Tao Master," Drakite said eventually. Katie-Anne and Adam broke apart.

"Don't you have any idea where the Tao Master is?" Katie-Anne asked hopefully, wiping tears away.

"No, I'm really sorry. Only the really high creatures will know. That would be the other sovereigns, and all of their apprentices and their high court." Katie-Anne looked suddenly disappointed.

"Couldn't you try and find it like this place?" she asked suddenly. Drakite smiled and shook his head.

"It's not as easy as that. The sovereigns don't live in this dimension. When they created life on this planet, they also created dimensional rips that would take them to dimensions that they created. You would have to do special things, things that I don't know, to get into their dimensions."

"But there has to be someone who-" Katie-Anne went into a sudden daze. A look of great excitement sprang onto her face.

"Drakite! Do you remember that bloke who told you to guard us? You know, the one we told you about, the one we met down the dark ally?"

"Yes," Drakite replied slowly.

"Could you bring him to us? Just tell him we need a lot of help finding one of the keys."

"But how could he possibly know?" Drakite replied.

"He is Poseidon's son. He might know something about travelling to their dimensions!" Adam suddenly grinned happily. Drakite grunted, but he still walked to the edge of the plateau.

"I don't know how long I will be, so be prepared for a long wait." With that, he opened his titanic wings and took off.

*

Katie-Anne didn't know how much time had passed, but they both just sat there waiting and waiting. Katie-Anne then took the book of Elementites out of her bag and began flicking through the pages.

"What are you doing?" Adam asked curiously.

"I'm looking up the Elementite we were just given. Apparently it's called 'The Cloudy Eye'. It unleashes something called 'White Mist'."

"Shame we can't use it, though," Adam replied.

"Yeah, I guess."

They spent the rest of the time watched clouds go by, then the sunset.

They were about to start to go to sleep when they heard the familiar flapping of Drakite's wings. Then, from bellow, up rose Drakite, with Solomon clinging to his neck. Drakite landed on the plateau and Solomon slipped off his back.

"What is it? What do you need help with?" he asked anxiously.

"Do you know who the Tao Master is?" Katie-Anne asked, trying to keep her voice calm.

"Of course I know who he is! I've met him a few times. He came to the christening of the Sphinxes," he replied casually.

"Do you know where he lives?" she asked anxiously. What if he didn't know?

"Why do you want to know?" he asked suspiciously.

"Because he got to the Sphinx's key before we could. We want to get to him, but we have no idea where to find him." The colour drained from Solomon's face. He ran his hand through his hair.

"Well, you wouldn't know where to find him - few do. But how do you know he has it?" he asked seriously.

"The Sphinx told us you idiot!" Adam shouted impatiently. "Can you help us or not?" Solomon looked at them, biting his upper lip.

"Alright. It might be tricky. There is no guarantee it will work, but I'll try my best." He turned to face Drakite. "Tragonzite. Can you fly us to China?" Drakite grunted angrily.

"I have a name you know! It's Drakite!" he grunted.

"Whatever. Can you take us to China?"

"Of course I can!" he answered as if this was an insulting question.

Solomon gripped Drakite around the neck. Katie-Anne clung around Solomon's waist and Adam clung around her waist. Drakite took off and plummeted downwards. Wind whistled painfully in their ears. Thankfully, they managed to avoid the clouds. Drakite then suddenly jolted left, his passengers clinging on for dear life.

Finally, they could see the bright lights from the continent of Asia.

"Tragonzite, can you fly us to Beijing?" Solomon shouted.

"Its Drakite!" he roared in return. However, he changed direction slightly and headed over the Chinese towns and cities. As they got closer to the ground, people kept pointing at them and gasping or else shouting in panic.

Darkness had really fallen now, and Drakite was finding it difficult to find a place to land.

"Where do you want me to land?" he asked.

"Don't! Fly high into the sky!" Solomon replied. Drakite darted upwards, wind howling around them, then "Stop!!" Solomon shouted suddenly. Drakite stopped efficiently. Solomon looked left and right, as though trying to sniff someone out.

"I can feel its presence," Solomon said randomly.

"The presence of what?" Adam asked. Solomon did not reply.

"Is 'its presence' a good thing, or a bad thing?" Katie-Anne asked. Yet again, Solomon chose not to reply, and kept looking around, as though he was trying to catch a scent.

Eventually, after a few minutes, Drakite grunted and lit the orb on his tail.

"Put out that light!" Solomon snapped at once. "I wont be able to see otherwise!" Katie-Anne and Adam exchanged amused looks.

"He's bonkers," Adam whispered. "How can turning off a light help you to see something in the darkness?" However, just as Adam finished speaking, Solomon began talking in a language none of them knew. Immediately, an orange light erupted from behind them. Then, a dim white light appeared in front of them. The orange light appeared to come from a small orb suspended in midair, about the size of a football. The dim white light also came from a small orb suspended in the air, but smaller; about the size of a tennis ball.

"What are they?" Katie-Anne asked nervously.

"The sun and the moon," replied Solomon happily.

"He really has gone bonkers!" replied Adam, not troubling to keep his voice down. Solomon just ignored him.

"I had a feeling he might keep them in disguise!" said Solomon proudly.

"What do you mean when you say they are the sun and the moon, Solomon?" Katie-Anne asked politely.

"The orange orb represents the sun, while the white orb shows the moon. It has been said that the sun, the goodness and the light that shines brightly above us, is the good half of the Tao. The moon, which also presents good qualities, is the bringer of darkness and evil."

"So what do we do with them now? What are they for?" Drakite asked impatiently.

"I think we need to bring them together, as one, to make the Tao. But I'm not sure how." After he finished talking to them, Solomon started muttering to himself, looking at the orbs, and sometimes pointing at them and talking in the weird language. However, nothing happened. "I think, this might work, but I can't be sure. Tragonzite, shine your tail in the direction of the moon." Drakite growled resentfully, but lit his tail and held it in the direction of the moon. As he lit his tail, the moon orb drifted to his tail. "Quick, Tragonzite! Fly to the sun and keep your tail held close to it!" Drakite complied. The moon still drifted towards them. Then, when it reached them, Drakite turned off his tail, and the moon drifted into the sun instead. Then they collided. An enormous bright white light shone momentarily as they fused, but quickly died away to reveal an orb that was the Tao. The two halves then swirled into each other and formed a vortex.

"How'd you know it was going to do that!?" asked Katie-Anne in amazement.

"Simple. The darkness is attracted to light, as the darkness desires nothing more that to obliterate the light. So, when a light as strong as the one on Drakite's tail is ignited, it couldn't resist. It was the only way to lure the two pieces together." Katie-Anne nodded, clearly impressed. Adam looked confused.

Drakite edged closer towards the vortex.

"Where will that take us?" Adam asked nervously.

"I trust you know that the sovereigns live in other dimensions?" Solomon asked seriously.

"Yes. Drakite told us, but-"

"This vortex takes us to the dimension in which the Tao Master lives. Once, all four sovereigns lived in the same dimension. But, unfortunately, it didn't end completely happily. Tiamat was the first to leave. She created another dimension, just for the darkest of all creatures. She felt impure to be around too much goodness. Mother Nature went next. Remember she married Father Time? Poseidon was the final one to leave. He built a dimension replicated from the sea. The Tao Master is the only one remaining in the original 'sovereign dimension'." Katie-Anne and Adam didn't know how to reply. "Anyway, enough going down memory lane. We need to get the next key. Tragonzite, fly as close as you can to the vortex." Drakite roared angrily.

"My name is DRAKITE!"

"Good for you. Just go, will you." Drakite hovered to the vortex. Katie-Anne could feel the vortex pulling on her, like a magnet pulls a metal pin.

Solomon leaped off Drakite's back and landed in the vortex. His outline distorted and he got smaller and smaller until he had vanished. Adam jumped off next. The same thing happened to him. Katie-Anne gulped.

"Is it painful?" she asked in a small voice.

"I don't think so. Just jump," Drakite replied. Katie-Anne gulped and jumped into the vortex. She felt a strange sensation. It felt like she was being sucked up by a vacuum cleaner, with hundreds of hands pushing her at all sides. All she could see was green light, with different coloured swirls every now and again.

Finally, the weird sensation ended and she felt as though she was falling through perpetual air. Then she landed, with a hard thump onto something solid. Katie-Anne looked up. She widened her eyes in shock. It was as though she had landed on the surface of Mars. The ground was completely compiled of red stone and dust, with many red hills and dunes. The sky looked as though it was at dusk. However, a moon was in one side of the sky, and a small dim sun was in the other.

Directly in front of her was a traditional Chinese building. The left hand side of the building was white, while the right hand side was black. The roof was as red as the landscape.

Solomon and Adam were standing a few feet away. Adam was staring very interestedly at the landscape and admiring the house. Solomon looked quite bored, as though he was in a queue in a super market. Seconds later, a small green rift appeared in the sky, and Drakite tumbled out and landed on the ground, sending red dust everywhere. Katie-Anne looked behind her, wondering how they would get back. She saw a small Tao suspended in the air. She supposed this must be the portal.

"I don't want to sound like an idiot, but where exactly are we, Mars?" Adam asked.

"This is not Mars, no. This dimension doesn't exist anywhere, it doesn't begin and it doesn't end," Solomon replied. Drakite, Katie-Anne and Adam didn't understand this in the slightest.

"It's very hard to explain. Our dimension is huge. There are hundreds of galaxies, and the universe doesn't end. Our dimension exists. It is where everything that begins and ends starts. Nothing happens here. It doesn't change; it stays like this forever. What you see here is all that is here. You can't go beyond the boundaries. Our dimension has no boundaries. A logical way of putting it is that this dimension is similar to that of a video game. It was created from our dimension. It can only be used for what it is designed for." Adam and Drakite still looked very confused, but Katie-Anne seemed to be grasping it.

"I see. So its like the Tao Master is the video programmer, and this is the world of the video game," Katie-Anne replied, "apart from the Tao Master can access his created world." Solomon smiled at her.

"Exactly. That is the simplest way I can put it. I'm sorry if it still doesn't make sense."

"Can he modify it as well?" she asked curiously.

"Whenever he wants. It didn't used to look like this. When he became the final sovereign to live here, he changed it to how he liked it. As you can see, he has decorated it to symbolise the Tao." Katie-Anne and Adam were very impressed. Katie-Anne never thought in her wildest dreams such places could exist.

"Come on. We are here for the key. Let's go in to the house," Solomon spoke when Katie-Anne and Adam showed interest in wanting to examine the landscape.

They all approached the building. The building was fairly high, and had double doors.

"Let's go in then," said Katie-Anne confidently. Solomon reached for the handles of the double doors and pushed them open. They creaked loudly. It was a little bit hard to see inside because there wasn't much light. The walls were a deep scarlet red in colour. The coving was coloured bright gold. Katie-Anne thought it might actually be made of gold the way it was shining. A picture of the moon was painted on the left wall and a picture of the sun was painted on the right wall.

However, none of it compared to what filled the back of the room. A small raised platform stood before them, and upon it lay a beautiful golden thrown. Above the thrown on the wall was a large coat of arms. It showed a phoenix bird with its wings above its head, and purple fire circling around it. The phoenix had the Tao symbol embedded on its breast. A banner made in silver below the Phoenix read: "*Nunquam stringo vox ventus*".

However, our hero's attention was only focused on the coat of arms very briefly, because sitting upon the golden thrown was a figure. The figure stayed stone still for a few moments then it jumped off the thrown, did a summersault in the air and landed before them.

The figure was dressed in a long white robe with a loincloth draped around his middle in gold velvet. The cloth had strange black symbols stitched into it. You could clearly see the figure's manly face, however his eyes were covered by a white hat (similar to a top hat) that sat on his head. He wore dark black boots, which were half covered by his white robe. His sleeves covered his hands, yet he held a long blue staff, which supported a glittering orb of the Tao.

A small image of the Tao was stitched onto the shoulders of the white robe and on the front of his hat.

"Why Solomon!" he said in a deep, powerful voice, "I haven't seen you for what? A few thousand years? How are you doing?"

"I'm fine thank you Tao Master," Solomon replied, bowing in respect.

"I see you brought some friends with you," he said merrily, as though they had arrived at some kind of party. "But why? Do you seek my help? My council?" he asked as though it was a very jolly occasion.

"We are here to recover the key you took from the Sky Sphinx," Solomon replied plainly. The Tao Master stopped laughing, his smile faltered.

"And why would you want the key?" replied the Tao Master, trying to suppress his annoyance.

"As I'm sure you know, the animals from the past are once again walking amongst us. If you didn't know, the Tragonzite behind us should be proof enough," Solomon answered, still in a plain unfaltering voice.

"But why would the monsters being unleashed drive you to recover the key?" he asked as though testing them. Of course the Tao Master knew, but he was just trying to make sure they were trustworthy enough.

"Tao Master, you have taken control over the good army we are trying to put together. You are doing this to combat the Manticore's growing evil army. You know that the Manticore is after Poseidon's powers, so you obtained one of the objects required in order for that to happen. As long as you have that key, it is unlikely the Manticore can ever get Poseidon's power. However, you forget that we need that key in order to lock away all the monsters of the past. If they stay, who knows what will happen to life on Earth. So we beg you, please, to give us that key. We will get to Poseidon's power and find the object that locks away the animals. We will then either destroy the keys or else hide them where no one can find them." The Tao Master listened intently, and when Solomon got to the bit about the possible destruction of life on Earth, he gave an uncomfortable jerk.

"Ok. I'm afraid I can't just give it away willingly. After all, I am its new protector," the Tao Master replied, no more his cheery self, but more serious.

"And as its protector, you should know better than anyone how important it is that these monsters are recaptured! You are the guardian of the balance of the world, yet *you* would willingly sit back and let it fall into catastrophe!" Solomon boomed argumentatively. The Tao Master's face bore a very ugly look at these words.

"And how do I know that if I give you the key, that it wont fall into the wrong hands!?" the Tao Master replied angrily, his voice rising.

"By looking at these!" Katie-Anne spoke at last. She drew out the two keys they had already obtained. The Tao Master goggled at them. "Tao Master. I can't guarantee that the keys won't be taken from us, but you have to trust us we will do whatever it takes to make sure we don't let them fall into evil hands. Please, I know you don't want the Manticore to get hold of the keys, and we are trying our best to prevent that. Just give us a chance to prove ourselves!" she gabbled desperately. The Tao Master turned his gazed in her direction, but Katie-Anne didn't know whether he was looking at her or not because his eyes were hidden.

"Right. I will give you a chance to prove yourselves. You must overcome one obstacle. You must prove that you are strong enough to look after the keys," he negotiated. "If one of you can successfully defend yourselves and survive twenty blows from me, then I will give you-" There was an almighty uproar. All of them protested:

"That is totally unjust-"

"You must be crazy-!"

"You can't honestly be serious-"

"Absolutely acrimonious -"

"Quiet!!" bellowed the Tao Master. Everyone fell silent immediately. "That is my final offer. Will you accept or not?" None of them said a word. Solomon looked at his companions then replied.

"Ok Tao Master, we will do it," he said uncomfortably.

Drakite, Katie-Anne and Adam turned away and began muttering angrily.

"Then decide amongst yourselves who will take on my challenge," replied the Tao Master. Katie-Anne, Adam, Solomon and Drakite huddled together.

"I could do it, I have a tough hide," Drakite murmured.

"But you don't have any powers to defend yourself with except fire. It's too risky. Besides, your wounds are still recovering from that other brutal attack by the Manticore's allies," Solomon hissed.

"Me or Adam could do it, we can defend ourselves with the power of earth," Katie-Anne whispered confidently.

"I can think of at least two things wrong with that," Solomon retorted. "Firstly, I don't think it would be fair to let you do it because you are a woman and you may not be able to defend yourself as effectively. Neither of you can do it anyway because the power of earth isn't going to be much good inside a building." Katie-Anne opened her mouth and gave Solomon a really offended look. His sexist remark had taken a worse blow than the Tao Master could ever inflict. She broke free of the group and stepped back a few paces and crossed her arms. Solomon looked at her for a few seconds then went back down into the huddle.

"I suppose it leaves me then, doesn't it?" Solomon said quietly.

"Have you decided yet?" the Tao Master asked impatiently.

"Yes, it will be me," replied Solomon, breaking away from the huddle and facing the Tao Master. The Tao Master gave half a smile.

"I had a feeling it might be." He looked at the others. "If you don't wish to be harmed, I would go stand near the thrown." They obeyed. All of them trotted along. Drakite and Adam were talking nervously, but Katie-Anne kept her mouth tightly shut, tears slightly trickling down her cheeks.

When the Tao Master was satisfied the others were a good distance away, he and Solomon faced each other.

"You may use whatever defence you feel is necessary. However, you can not attack me directly." He pointed his staff and Solomon. "Get ready now." The orb of the Tao on top of the staff became pearly white.

Then a large, 3D star-shaped beam boomed out. Solomon stuck his hand out in front of him and a red shield spread from his palm and surrounded his body like a bubble. The beam struck the bubble and made a sound like hammer hitting metal. The red bubble started to indent and Solomon's face became more pained. Then the star-beam stopped. Solomon stopped the bubble. He was panting like he had just run for his life.

It then happened three more times. The Tao Master used the same unchanging star-beam, and Solomon kept with his red bubble. As the attempts went on, he got weaker, and so did his bubble.

On the fifth attack, the beam finally punctured the bubble. It struck Solomon hard in the chest. He yelled loudly and was thrown into the air. He landed in a heap on the floor near the doors. He got up slowly, holding his arm.

"Come on Solomon! I know you can do better than this! You're probably out of practice."

"You're enjoying this, aren't you!?" Solomon shouted angrily. The Tao Master shook his head.

"Solomon, we have barely begun. I'm not even trying, and I've already got to you on the fifth attack. You still have fifteen to go." Solomon chose not to reply. The Tao Master pointed his staff again. In the split second before he fired, Solomon waved his hands at the doors and they flew open. The Tao Master shot another beam. Solomon put both his hands in front of him and the beam stopped just short of them. His hands we being forced back through the shear power of the beam. Solomon narrowed his eyes at the beam and it began to change direction. He then forced his hands to his right and the beam changed direction and shot through the open door and exploded on a sand dune.

"I'm impressed! Using psychic powers to change direction of the beam! You must be very advanced at telekinesis to do that!" boomed the Tao Master clearly impressed.

"I do my best," Solomon replied proudly.

The Tao Master kept on using the star-beam, and Solomon used numerous counter-attacks to defend himself. By the seventeenth attack he started to get really weak.

"Hang in there Solomon! Only three more attacks!" Adam shouted encouragingly. On the eighteenth attack, Solomon fired a silver beam from his hand as the star-beam left the Tao Master's staff. The two beams clashed and formed a small energy ball. The same thing happened on the nineteenth attack.

"Well done Solomon, you've reached the last blast. I'm going to turn the power up a bit. Prepare yourself." He pointed his staff for the last time. Instead of going pearly white, the orb shone red. A red ring began circling the orb, then a second red ring, then a third. The three rings launched from the staff. Solomon raised his hands into the air. A large blue energy ball formed. He then brought his hands down and threw the orb at the rings. When they clashed an almighty eruption took place. Solomon was thrown backwards and smashed into the painting of the moon on the wall. Where he hit the wall, there was now a large crack. An enormous crater was in the floor where the two attacks collided.

Solomon got up carefully, one side of his face bleeding. He put his hand on his back.

"Bravo!" boomed the Tao Master, who was completely unscathed. "Well done! You completed the task successfully. I will keep my side of the bargain and give you your reward." The Tao Master walked to his thrown and opened a camouflaged hatch on the small raised platform. He pulled out a small purple orb. The key. He faced the trio standing at the back of the thrown. The Tao Master held the orb out in his free hand. Katie-Anne took it.

"Thank you," she said gratefully, doing a small respectful bow.

"Keep this safe. The Manticore must not get hold of the keys, or it might literally be the end of the world, as we know it. Get to the power before he does."

"We will do our best," replied Adam.

"Humans! Before you go I would like to give a gift," said the Tao Master, as they were about to walk away. Katie-Anne and Adam exchanged puzzled looks.

"Why would you give us gifts, we haven't done anything to deserve them," Adam replied confused.

"I want to reward you for obtaining three of the keys. Its exceptionally hard for humans who don't know much about what they are doing to even find the resting place of one key, no matter actually finding three. It must take extraordinary talent to accomplish that feat."

"Well, thank you very much Tao Master," replied Katie-Anne blushing slightly.

"Erm, Tao Master? I think it should only be Katie-Anne who deserves that gift, because she was the one who managed to solve all the riddles. I have barely helped at all," Adam said awkwardly. The Tao Master shook his head and smiled.

"No young Adam. You have helped on this quest, ways you don't know yet. I'd say you are essential." Adam smiled modestly. "You deserve the gift as much as Katie-Anne. And if I might say so, I think it is a gift you will both thoroughly enjoy." Both Katie-Anne and Adam look excited.

"Now, as I understand it, both of you have been gifted to control the element of earth?" he asked. Both of them nodded. "Stay still." He raised his hand into the air. Then a wind began blowing inside the room. Adam and Katie-Anne were then engulfed in a small gust. For a moment, Katie-Anne's lungs froze and she couldn't breath. However, she could feel a strange chilly wind entering them and pass into her body. Then it all ended. The gust finished and Katie-Anne and Adam could breathe again.

"I have gifted you with the power of the sky. You can now control the element of wind, as well as that of earth. This power will help you in your battles ahead. Good luck!"

"Th-th-thank you!" Katie-Anne stammered.

"Yeah, thank you so much," Adam replied as though he couldn't believe what just happened.

The party of four left the house and opened the portal back to their dimension. Katie-Anne was so happy; she even forgot to be angry with Solomon. Then it was her turn to enter. Yet again she felt the sensation of being pulled into a vacuum cleaner. Finally, they were back.

Chapter 11
The Defender of the Deep

When Katie-Anne flew out of the vortex, she had nothing to land on and fell through the air, screaming, until Drakite flew underneath her and caught her. Solomon and Adam were already on his back.

"Thanks Drakite," she gasped.

"No problem." Drakite gave an enormous flap of his wings and took off. It was no longer night time here; it looked as though it was the middle of the day.

"So we have three keys! Just the water and fire keys left!" said Adam excitedly.

"I don't think any of us are in any condition to go searching for another key today. We should rest up and look tomorrow," Drakite growled.

"Are you going to come with us when we search for the remaining keys?" Katie-Anne asked Solomon.

"I don't think I will be able to. I have things I need to do," he replied as though he was vaguely temped by the offer.

"What kind of things?" Adam asked curiously.

"None that concern you for the time being," Solomon replied plainly.

Once they had found a nice open clearing where it was unlikely they could be spotted, Drakite landed and his passengers tumbled off.

"Well, I'll be off!" said Solomon, yawning and stretching. He closed his eyes and disappeared in a cloud of blue smoke.

*

After a few minutes rest, Adam and Katie-Anne climbed back onto Drakite and he took them back to England and landed round a corner close to where Katie-Anne lived. They said goodbye to him and he took off and disappeared. Katie-Anne and Adam walked round the corner. When Katie-Anne saw her house she gasped. There was a crowd of around a hundred people there, mostly journalists and news reporters.

"How on earth are we going to get through this lot?" she asked Adam, shacking her head.

"We're going to have to barge through," Adam replied, a slight glimmer of laughter in his voice. So they cautiously set off for her house. When they were about sixty yards away, someone screamed, "That's them!" and all the journalists and reporters hurried off to meet them. Katie-Anne and Adam felt themselves having random questions probed at them, and cameramen calling their names to get a good shot. Katie-Anne followed Adams advice and pushed through the crowd and quickly unlocked her door. Just before Adam came in, Katie-Anne spotted her mother in the crowd. She was being shoved aside by the reporters, her curly brown hair knocked everywhere. Katie-Anne ran back out of the house, grabbed her mum and rushed back inside, where she swiftly locked the door. As soon as they were inside, Katie-Anne's mother burst into tears and hugged Katie-Anne, who cried as well.

"Why did you not tell me!" her mother wailed, "I've been worried sick, you could have died! Anything could have happened to you!"

"Mum, I'm fine, don't worry. Adam and I-" at his name, her mother broke free from Katie-Anne and gazed at Adam. She flung herself onto him instead.

"Thank you so much for protecting her! I don't know what I would have done if she died!" she sobbed.

"Adam, this is my mother, Wendy Springwood." Wendy let go of Adam and shook his hand.

"Katie-Anne, I want you to tell me everything that has happened since you left for Brazil, please," Wendy asked. Katie-Anne beckoned her mother to sit down and her and Adam began telling her mother what had happened. Wendy wanted to interrupt but Katie-Anne continued with the story.

"What do you mean when you say you can control earth and wind?" she asked blankly.

"Well, we need to go outside to show you," Adam replied. So they trotted off into the back garden and Katie-Anne raised a large chunk of earth from the garden and began forming it into weird shapes above their heads. Then Adam formed a strong gust, which he turned into a harmless mini-tornado. At the sight of the powers, Wendy fainted.

Adam and Katie-Anne carefully laid Wendy down on one of the sofas.

"It will break her heart when we have to go and find another key," Katie-Anne said to Adam sadly.

"It has to be done. Talking of which, I wonder when Drakite will find the next key?"

Later on that day, Wendy went home and Katie-Anne and Adam spent the rest of the day resting. The next morning, there was an almighty thump on the front door.

"If its them stupid reporters again I'll-" Katie-Anne opened the door and Drakite was standing outside.

"Drakite! Hello!" said Katie-Anne, as though she was greeting someone to a dinner party. "I would ask you to come in, but I don't think you will fit."

"That's fine, because we're leaving soon. Solomon told me the whereabouts of the next key."

"I presume it is the water key because I think we all know that the fire key is at the statue of the Sphinx. Anyway, it has to be the water key."

"Why does it have to be the water key?" Drakite growled.

"Because the Desert Sphinx told us she would not give us her key until we had the other four. Anyway, where is the location of the next key?"

"Under the Pacific Ocean, directly underneath the equator." Adam walked into the room, still half asleep.

"Reporters at this hour?" he mumbled.

"No Adam. Get dressed, we're going to get the next key!"

*

After a very quick breakfast they were all set to go. They climbed onto Drakite and they were off.

"Drakite? Katie-Anne told me that you told her that Solomon told you that the key is in the Pacific Ocean. Well, for one how are we meant to breath and two, the Pacific is huge!" Adam said rather matter-of-factly. Katie-Anne's stomach dropped. *How* were *they mean to breath?*

'Don't worry about that, when it comes to it, we will find a way," Drakite replied confidently. A smile crept up on his face and his voice was a bit more bubbly than usual.

"Drakite, are you hiding something from us?" Katie-Anne asked suspiciously.

"I'm saying no more, I don't want to spoil the surprise."

"Surprise?" Adam whispered. Katie-Anne shrugged.

Eventually, they left the United Kingdom far behind and were already midway through the Caribbean Sea.

"Not far now. Only about an hour or so and we will be right above the Pacific Ocean!" Drakite roared happily. Soon enough they were there. It was just endless water; no landmass could be spotted anywhere. Drakite then stopped abruptly, and stayed aloft in midair.

"I think this is roughly the place," he said casually.

"How do you know? It could be anywhere around this place," Katie-Anne asked, gazing at the endless blanket of water.

"Trust me." Drakite took a deep breath and shot a fireball into the water. An enormous splash of water exploded.

"What did you do that for?" Adam asked angrily.

"Wait, and you will see." At that moment several heads protruded above the water, one after the other until there was about three-dozen. Katie-Anne and Adam almost fell off Drakite's back in surprise. They were people, but they were underwater! Then several different coloured fins cut through the water below the heads of the people. Katie-Anne understood. *They are merpeople!*

When the merpeople spotted the humans, they began cheering and flapping around happily.

"Drakite, why are they so happy to see us?" Katie-Anne asked slightly angrily, knowing Drakite had concealed something from them.

"Well, yesterday, I found out there is a sea monster underneath here that has been terrorising the merpeople. I had a chat with the merpeople, and I promised them that if they would be willing to give the power the breath underwater, I would bring them their saviour-"

"You did what!?" Adam thundered.

"Why Drakite? Why?" Katie-Anne asked disbelievingly.

"Just calm down. This is the only way. We need powers to breath underwater to get the key. We can also kill two birds with one stone this way. The key should be directly beneath here, and if you can get the power to control water as well, it's a bonus. It is either this, or no key at all! What will it be?" Katie-Anne and Adam looked at each other apprehensively.

"We've got no choice, have we?" said Adam quietly.

"What do they expect us to do?" Katie-Anne asked nervously.

"They want you to scare the beast away, and make sure it never terrorises them again," Drakite replied, a little happier now Katie-Anne and Adam were coming to the terms of the idea. "Basically, I'm going to fly you down to the merpeople, and you jump into the water. They will then give you the power to breath. Ok?" Both of them nodded. With that, Drakite flew all the way down and Adam and Katie-Anne jumped in. They both gasped in shock. The water was incredibly cold, and their clothes were weighing them down. The merpeople swam as close as they could to Katie-Anne and Adam and some of them put their slimy hands upon Katie-Anne and Adam. Katie-Anne felt a strange tingling feeling, as though water was passing through her insides. It soon stopped.

"So we can now breathe underwater?" Katie-Anne asked, as the merpeople withdrew their hands.

"You can breathe, talk, swim better than you can walk, and you can control the water element, just like you can control earth and wind!" Drakite replied, beaming at them.

"What do we do now? Dive under?" Adam asked.

"Exactly. The merpeople will lead you once you go under," Drakite replied confidently. So Katie-Anne and Adam kicked off their shoes and watched them sink. They pulled off all loose clothing and they were ready to dive.

"Ready?" Katie-Anne asked nervously.

"When you are," Adam replied. Together, they bobbed up then dived down. Katie-Anne realised the cold wasn't effecting her very much anymore. Then she realised she wasn't breathing through her mouth. She tried but it was like her larynx and windpipe had been sealed off. Instead, she could feel the oxygen vaporising through her chest into her lungs. The sensation was very similar to the sensation you got by putting on Vick.

As soon as they were underwater, the merpeople swam down, their great fins beating behind them. Katie-Anne felt the unusual instinct to swim in a serpent-like fashion. She moved easily through the water, with Adam on her left, swimming in a similar way to sharks.

When they had got quite deep, the merpeople stopped and one of them turned around and talked to Katie-Anne.

"The beast will be here at any moment," the merman said quite seriously. Katie-Anne opened her eyes wide in shock. It was weird seeing someone talking underwater. "If we swim beyond here and get any closer to that rock formation, it will attack." The merman spoke in a very echoic voice, as if it was talking with special effects. Katie-Anne wanted to reply, but she wasn't sure if it would work. She thought and expected bubbles to issue from her mouth. But her voice carried out in the same echoic tone.

"What is the sea monster exactly? And why will it attack if you get too close to that rock formation?" she asked curiously.

"The beast is a Hydra. The rock formation has a small cavern. We have no idea what is inside, as none who have tried to enter have ever got by. Please, you must beat the Hydra." Katie-Anne felt her stomach disappear, and she felt an icy chill creep down her neck that had nothing to do with the chill of the water.

"The Hy-Hy-Hydra?" she murmured petrified.

"What kind of monster is the Hydra?" Adam asked, looking straight into Katie-Anne's horrified eyes.

"It is a vicious sea demon. It is a cross between a sea dinosaur and a whale. The creature has nine powerful heads. Every time one head is destroyed, it grows back, more powerful than before," she replied, unable to keep the fear from her voice. Adam shrunk away, shaking his head.

"But, how can we beat it?" Katie-Anne asked the merpeople, as though she was pleading for an answer.

"I'm afraid we don't know," replied one of the merpeople. Gloom seamed to settle upon them. "All who have tried have perished. The Hydra is truly cannibalistic. We don't wish to frighten you, but prepare you for what lies ahead."

"We're doomed Katie-Anne. We can't beat this thing," Adam said desperately.

"We have to try. If we don't, we can't get the forth key. After all, we do have the power to control three elements. The Hydra might be frightened easily by them." Adam just stared at the rock formation. Even though they had swum quite far down, the sunlight still penetrated the water this far down, and the rock was glimmering beautifully in the light.

"Ok then. We will do it," Adam replied bravely. "I think you merpeople should take cover, we don't want you getting injured." The merpeople murmured in agreement and went to take cover amongst corals and rocks. Katie-Anne and Adam grasped hands and swam towards the big rock formation. They could see a small dent where they supposed the cavern must be. As they got closer, they saw loads of fantastically wonderful rare corals and colourful fish. Katie-Anne even spotted a mythical animal in the distance, a Capricorn; a goat with a fin of a dolphin. As Katie-Anne was about to point it out, when they heard an angry marine-growl. The fish darted away quickly, and the Capricorn swam away as fast as it could. A giant shadow was moving below them. Katie-Anne and Adam went back to back, both shaking.

"It must be the Hydra," Katie-Anne whispered. Then suddenly something large shot past them as fast as a rocket. The vibration waves were so powerful Katie-Anne and Adam were swept away and they collided painfully with the rock formation. The Hydra then appeared before them. It was the most evil specimen Katie-Anne ever saw. She thought the Chimera was evil, but the Hydra had gained its title. The Hydra was a deep blue in colour. Its body was identical to a plesiosaur. It had nine similar elongated heads that looked like crosses between a dragon and a venomous snake. All the way round its body, the Hydra bore strange metallic turquoise zigzag stripes. The beast's florescent blue eyes bulged at the sight of them.

One of the beast's heads took a deep breath and let forth a large spiral jet of water. Katie-Anne and Adam just managed to swim out of the way in time as the attack struck the rock formation, making chunks of sharp shards fall. Adam whipped his left hand at the Hydra and a vine-like whip burst from his palm and tied itself around one of the Hydra's necks like a lasso. The head began to struggle in anger. As two of the heads tried to bite the trapped head free, the six remaining heads looked at Adam murderously.

Katie-Anne decided it was time to test her new powers. She pointed her fingers at the Hydra and icicles shot out of them and cut through the water like torpedoes. They pierced the Hydra's skin easily on impact. The creature thrashed around in anger and pain. Another head opened its mouth and let loose water balls the size of cannon balls. They caught Katie-Anne in the stomach one after the other. She clutched her stomach as though she was winded and she fell unconscious and began to float.

"NO!!" Adam bellowed as he watched Katie-Anne's lifeless body float eerily. He was the only one left fighting. His eyes flashed blue and an enormous pump of water burst from his mouth. The Hydra was struck hard. It was struck so hard it was actually forced through the water and smashed into the rock formation. The Hydra's skin was extremely bruised where Adam's attack struck and it was bleeding from where it hit the rock. All the heads sent a pulse of water towards Adam. Adam concentrated on his wind powers and tried to make a tornado, before remembering he was underwater. However, the tornado formed into a giant whirlpool. The Hydra's attacks were sucked into it and disappeared. Adam clung onto a coral to stop himself getting pulled in. He watched in horror as the lifeless Katie-Anne was being pulled in. As she went by, Adam grabbed her arm. The Hydra tried to swim away but it was too late. It was pulled in and it zoomed around and around. Adam subsided the whirlpool and the Hydra was thrown out like it had been catapulted. Yet again it smashed into the rock formation. This time, a lot of the rock gave way and the Hydra fell to the bottom, with the giant rock crumbling on top.

Adam immediately turned his attention to Katie-Anne. He put his finger on her neck and he could definitely feel a pulse. She was alive. Then, she began opening her eyes as though she had been in a deep sleep.

"Adam?" she whispered weak and confused.

"Yes, I'm here. You're ok now. The Hydra is gone." The merpeople began reappearing in all directions cheering heartily.

"Thank you, human. You have saved us from a great atrocity. We are forever in your dept," said what appeared to be the head merman. He bowed deeply, followed by the others.

"So what do we do now?" Adam asked.

"The Tragonzite told us that you were looking for some sort of treasure to do with the Sphinx. We have no sources or evidence, but we suspect the cavern might hold what you desire," spoke the head merman.

"Thank you. Just be careful for the future. The Hydra may return." The merpeople all bowed again then swam away. Adam took a firm grip around Katie-Anne and swam down to the cavern. As he swam by a coral, he noticed something shining within it. He put his hand into the coral and pulled out a weird object that was shaped like a droplet, and it appeared to be made of glass. If he didn't know better, it was an Elementite; the first water Elementite they had found. Adam pocketed it and swam to the entrance of the cave. It was extremely dark inside. Adam was thinking longingly of the light on Drakite's tail, which was miles above him and no good to him. Adam swam into the cave, keeping very close to the wall of the cave so he could feel his way. Eventually, he bumped into a dead end. However, there was a bracket on the wall with a very dark blue flame. Adam laughed at this. *There was fire underwater!*

His thoughts immediately strayed to the cave in the Alps where there was a bracket on the wall then with a similar flame. This was a good sign that this cavern might just be the lair of the Sphinx.

Underneath the blue flame, there was a strange symbol shaped like a whirlpool. Adam yet again remembered in the cave in the Alps when Drakite had made the Kobalticle use its ice powers to create the door. Adam wondered weather he should do the same with his waterpowers. He pointed his free hand at the symbol and let out a small jet of water. It touched the symbol gently. At once it began glowing brightly and the wall began to lift up.

Chapter 12
Return of the Manticore

Adam swam through the new doorway. The water inside was very shallow. He stuck his head above water. At once, the feeling of vapour passing into his chest vanished, and he could breathe through his mouth again. This sudden change made him cough. Next to him, Katie-Anne began coughing as well. She opened her eyes again. She still looked fairly dazed.

"Are you ok?" he asked her seriously. She shook her head violently and looked as though she had just come out of a trance.

"Yes, yes I'm fine," she replied, sweeping her saturated hair out of her face. "Are we here? Is this it?"

"I think so, but we will have to see," Adam replied, looking around the room they had just entered. It was really small and damp. More brackets hung on the dark stone walls lit with the same brilliant blue flames. There was a small pond next to them full of completely clear water.

"So you have arrived!" came a voice from the back of the room. The speaker walked into the open where Katie-Anne and Adam could see. It was the Sphinx. She looked exactly like her sisters except she had a slight tinge of blue in her colour.

"I'm amazed you managed to pass the test," she said happily.

"What test?" Adam asked sounding very puzzled.

"The test of strength my dear lad! You defeated my guardian, the defender of the deep, the Hydra!" the Sphinx replied.

"The Hydra...was yours?" Adam asked incredulously.

"Yes of course. I'll explain. I have never been as good as my sisters at coming up with riddles. So instead, I appointed a guardian to defend me. However, it didn't go exactly the way I planned it. The Hydra has been attacking those who do not wish to come here. I might sack him." Adam and Katie-Anne exchanged exasperated looks. "So the key, my friends, is yours"

"Are-are you sure? That's all we had to do?" Katie-Anne asked, just making sure she heard correctly.

"Yes, are you slow on the uptake? Here it is!" she opened her paw and it held out small dark blue orb. Katie-Anne and Adam jumped out of the water. They approached the Sphinx cautiously, still unsure.

"Don't be afraid me dears. You have done your part," said the Sphinx, smiling merrily. Katie-Anne reached out her hand and took the orb from her paw.

"Before you go, please drink from the magical pond of Brothrin. It will replenish your strength, your energy and your powers. It will heal your wounds," said the Sphinx, pointing to the pond of clear water Adam noticed earlier. Katie-Anne and Adam walked over to the pond and took it in turns to have a drink. From the moment the liquid poured down their throats, they felt a strong surge of energy rush through them. All their aches and pains vanished.

"Thank you Sphinx," said Adam gratefully.

"How does the water do that?" Katie-Anne asked inquisitively.

"The water comes from the legendary Lady of the Lake," the Sphinx told. Katie-Anne gasped.

"The Lady of the Lake! She's real!?" Katie-Anne interrupted unbelievingly.

"Yes. She hides herself far away. She is the only one who can brew a special brand of water to heal. Not even Poseidon could do it. The water is called the Brothrin, but we don't know why. I knew that fighting the Hydra would greatly injure anyone who managed to get here, so I asked the Lady of the Lake if she would supply some of her Brothrin water to me, and she did." Katie-Anne took this news as a real treat.

"Wow! Where does she live?" Katie-Anne asked in awe.

"I'm sorry but I don't know. The Lady of the Lake is an extremely powerful immortal and she guards herself from threats. In fact, she is so powerful, creatures wanted her to be the next water sovereign."

"That is amazing," Katie-Anne replied ecstatically. "Adam, if we ever get time, I want to try and find the Lady of the Lake." Adam looked puzzled.

"If you want to," he replied.

"Anyway, we'd better by off. There is just one more thing. Sphinx, is it possible to take a bottle of this Brothrin water just in case we might need it in the future?" Katie-Anne asked hopefully. The Sphinx looked at her for a moment before replying.

"I can't see the harm," she replied calmly.

"Excellent!" Adam replied. Katie-Anne dived into her soaking rucksack and tried to find and empty bottle.

"Why don't you use this instead," the Sphinx suggested, holding out a small, beautifully shaped crystal phial.

"What's special about that phial?" Katie-Anne asked, abandoning her search.

"It will never break, and it will only let its true user drink from it," the Sphinx replied. "This will stop anything undesirable drinking the Brothrin water."

"But if it only lets its true user drink from it, it will only let you drink from it, wont it?" Katie-Anne asked uncertainly.

"No. Once it has been handed down to someone under the owner's free will, it will belong to that person. However, if it is taken by force or duress, it will not allow the thief to drink. Understand?"

"Yes. How does it do that?" Katie-Anne asked in amazement.

"Poseidon invented it, so I don't know how it works. It is the only object of his that wasn't locked away." Katie-Anne took it gently from the Sphinx, feeling honoured. She couldn't believe that she now owned something that used to belong to the creator of water, one of the four strongest beings.

"Thank you so much," Katie-Anne stammered. Adam walked closer to her to look at the phial. They walked back over to the Magical Pond of Brothrin, and Katie-Anne scooped up some of the water into the phial, and sealed it with a crystal cork.

"Thank you for everything, Sphinx. We need to be on our way," Adam said gratefully.

"Take care, and good luck!" the Sphinx replied. Katie-Anne and Adam slid into the shallow depths and both felt the sensation of vapour entering their lungs through their chests. They swam swiftly back through the dark cavern and back into the wide Pacific Ocean. The merpeople were waiting for them.

"Well? What was in there?" the head merman asked anxiously. Katie-Anne and Adam told them what had transpired.

"So the Sphinx *does* live in that cavern. At least we can stop being curious about it now," spoke one of the other mermen.

The merpeople escorted Katie-Anne and Adam as they swam back to the surface. When they surfaced, Katie-Anne and Adam smiled at each other, when they heard loud thunderous roars, and the beating of huge wings. They looked up. Drakite was fighting a large red lion that bore a venomous green scorpion sting, and large bat-like skeletal wings. The lion's blood red mane was a lot longer and bushier than a normal lion's mane. Katie-Anne recognised it immediately, even though she had never seen one before. It was a Manticore. Katie-Anne couldn't be one hundred percent sure it was the one they had been trying to thwart, but then why else would a Manticore be here in the middle of the Pacific Ocean.

Drakite let out a burst of lilac fire just as peridot coloured fire erupted from the Manticore's mouth. The two fire breaths clashed and formed a fireball. Drakite spotted Katie-Anne and Adam, broke free from the fire conflict and flew closer to them. He stared at them fearfully.

"Dive back down, NOW! Protect the keys; get away-" he managed to shout before the Manticore tackled him. The Manticore then turned to face the pair. He dived at them. Katie-Anne and Adam hurried underwater and swam down as fast as they could. The Manticore's paws groped the surface of the water in vain. Katie-Anne, Adam and the merpeople could see its shadow circling above them. After a while it flew off. They all waited underwater for a few minutes to make sure that it was truly gone.

Katie-Anne grew extremely worried about Drakite. He was up there, probably injured and weak, and the Manticore could still be attacking him. She decided to swim up.

"Katie-Anne, wait!" Adam shouted after her.

"Drakite needs our help!" she shouted back. Adam followed her, and behind him so did the merpeople. Katie-Anne cautiously stuck her head above water and looked around. The Manticore was nowhere in sight. Drakite was flying awkwardly above her before falling down into the water.

"Drakite!" Katie-Anne shouted desperately. Adam and the merpeople surfaced just as she swam to meet Drakite. He had numerous burns and injuries all the way around his body. One of his wings had a tear.

"Drakite, what did he do to you?" she asked, venom and righteous anger pouring into her body.

"I'm fine, I just need a rest. I'll be fine in a minute," he replied weakly. Adam's face swiftly turned angry and Katie-Anne had never seen him look so enraged.

"When we meet that Manticore again," he thundered, "I'm going to show about as much mercy as he deserves! NONE! I will destroy him!"

"Adam, you won't be able to, none of us will. He is extremely powerful. He seems to have grown even stronger than what he was before. Think how powerful he is now. He will be unstoppable if he gets to Poseidon's power," Drakite said reasonably. "We need to concentrate on getting the final key, and quick." He shot back up into the air.

"Drakite, I don't think you're in any condition to fly," Katie-Anne spoke anxiously.

"I'm fine, I'm a dragon. I'm designed to fight and survive attacks like this. Come on, climb on my back." He hovered above the water and Katie-Anne and Adam jumped on. They bid farewell to the merpeople and they were off. Katie-Anne and Adam explained everything that had happened since they met the Hydra.

"Then the Sphinx gave us a crystal phial she said Poseidon owned and we took some of the Brothrin water. Then we swam back out and saw you being mutilated by the Manticore," Katie-Anne told. Drakite was very interested in the phial but dropped the conversation quickly.

"That reminds me. Katie-Anne, when we land, can I have a look at the Elementite book?" Adam asked.

"Why?" she asked suspiciously.

"When you were unconscious, I think I found an Elementite," he replied.

"Oh can see!" she replied excitedly. Adam dug in his pocket and took out the glass drop. Katie-Anne really liked it.

"Ok, we'll see what power it contains when we land," said Katie-Anne, still admiring the drop.

Drakite flew so quickly they were back in the Sahara in an hour.

"So the Desert Sphinx was the first one you met, wasn't she?" Drakite asked, as they got closer to the statue.

"Yes. In fact, she was the first mythical animal we met," Katie-Anne replied reminiscing. The statue came into view in the distance, a dark silhouette in the setting sun. But as they got closer, Katie-Anne realised something was not right. The statue was a lot smaller then what it was last time. When they eventually landed beside it, it looked worse-for-wear. Its back had crumbled down a lot and a large chunk of the already damaged face had been slashed off.

"What happened to it?" Katie-Anne asked in shock, just staring at it.

"You don't think the Manticore got here first, do you?" Adam asked Drakite anxiously.

"I certainly hope not," Drakite replied fearfully.

"Well, it's a shame that I did, isn't it?" came a dark growl from behind the statue. Katie-Anne felt an icy prickle of fear go down her spine. A beast leapt up from the back of the statue and landed before them. It was the Manticore. He was gripping the Sphinx in his front paws. She was tied up thick binding ropes. Her paws were bound together and she had a cloth stuffed in her throat. Her scorpion sting was tied to her back. She was struggling against them desperately. The Manticore pointed his sting at her throat.

"Now, give me the keys, and I let her go," he said maliciously.

"You foul, evil, twisted monster!" Katie-Anne shouted savagely, "You would tie up and kill your own daughter to gain immortality!?"

"She means nothing to me! She is just a another worthless organism that is persistent in getting in my way!" the Manticore replied ferociously. "But no more!" He drew out one of his paws and he held out a small red orb. The key.

"She would not give me the key willingly, so I had to torture it out of her. Don't make me do the same to you!"

"Like you care who you have to hurt or step over to get what you want. You'll do away with us once we give you the keys anyway!" Katie-Anne spat boldly.

"You are messing with powers you can't possibly comprehend!" the Manticore thundered.

"If you want the keys, come and get them!" Adam bellowed.

"With pleasure," the Manticore replied politely, yet seriously. The Manticore threw the Sphinx from him. She crashed onto the sand, still struggling against the ropes that bound her. The Manticore lunged. Katie-Anne fired a cauliflower bomb, but the Manticore swiped it away easily with one of his paws. Adam began spinning around like a spinning-top and formed into a whirlpool. The whirlpool zoomed towards the Manticore. The Manticore let loose an immense burst of fire, reducing the whirlpool to steam. Adam fell to the ground. Drakite's tanzanite horns on his head began to spark and he fired a bolt of blue electricity from them. The Manticore placed the tip of his tail into the sand. The electricity passed through him into the ground, barely injuring him.

The Manticore dived at Adam, knocking him flying. He then dived towards Katie-Anne. He picked her up with one of his paws and dropped her from twenty feet in the air. She landed with a thump. All the contents from her bag spilled everywhere, including the keys. Drakite charged towards the Manticore and they began battling in the air. Drakite let out a blast of purple fire. The Manticore evaded it and tackled Drakite with similar force to that of a train. Drakite collided with the ground, sending sand everywhere.

"Now I can claim my prize!" the Manticore boomed delightedly. Katie-Anne, Adam and Drakite were too injured to do much.

The Manticore landed next to Katie-Anne, wiped her out of the way, and then picked up all the keys they had spent so hard trying to find.

"Finally! Poseidon's power *will* be mine!" He took off. Katie-Anne pointed her hand at the sand and whipped up a tornado. The sand got caught in the tornado turning it into a sandstorm. But it did no good. When it ended, the Manticore was gone.

Chapter 13
Poseidon's Sovereignty

Adam (who was closest to the Sphinx) crawled to her and untied her. The Sphinx got to her feet, looking worried and shaken.

"This is the worst thing that could possibly happen!" she said fearfully. "The Manticore has all the keys!! He will get to Poseidon's power first!"

"Don't worry, we will do everything in our power to stop him!" Katie-Anne replied confidently, getting to her feet and nursing an injured arm.

"We will need all the help we can get. I will alert my sisters, the Tao Master and Solomon. You need to give chase to the Manticore and divert him from getting to the powers before backup arrives," the Sphinx ordered. "You will need more fire power, literally. I will grant you the power of fire." The Sphinx reared onto her hind legs, looking powerful and impressive. She placed her front paws on Katie-Anne and Adam's shoulders. Katie-Anne felt a pleasant sensation of something warm licking her insides. She felt a lurch of untraceable power surge through her, and then it ended.

"The Manticore will be heading towards Stonehenge, because that is were the keys react to unlock Poseidon's treasure," the Sphinx recited. She turned to Drakite. "Tragonzite, you will need to fly them there as soon as possible and as fast as you can!" Drakite winced at being called 'Tragonzite' but nodded to show he understood. The Sphinx extended her brilliant feathery wings and took off into the sky. She flew a lot faster then what Drakite could.

"Are you sure you're ok to fly Drakite?" Adam asked, looking anxiously at the many wounds and injuries covering Drakite's ruined scales.

"I'm fine, we just need to concentrate on getting to Stonehenge," he replied. Katie-Anne and Adam quickly clambered onto Drakite's back and he took off. He flew as fast as he could, zooming around in the air.

It took them about an hour to get back to Britain and into Stonehenge. It was a dreadful sight. The road near the formation was littered with crashed and destroyed and burning cars. Trees had been ripped up or set alight. The ropes surrounding Stonehenge had been torn down. The place was devoid of active life, except right in the centre of Stonehenge. The Manticore stood inside the old columns of Stonehenge, the keys placed in a circle around him. Now that all the keys were together, they were flashing.

"I'm glad you could make it to my Power-rebirth party. You will see the extraordinary strength, which will be placed upon me. I will be almost indestructible! In my new form, I will hunt down the remaining three sovereigns and take their powers too! I will be unstoppable-"

"You are delusional!" bellowed Katie-Anne.

"That will never happen!" Drakite roared. The Manticore laughed patronisingly at them.

"Go on then. Here, have a free shot," the Manticore said jokily. "Or would you like to fight me one last time? How about this, if you beat me, I will disappear forever. If you lose, then the power is mine. Deal?"

"We will never make that deal with you!" Adam shouted vehemently. Drakite looked disdainfully at the Manticore.

"Fair enough. But don't say I didn't offer. Now, either stand back and watch me grow to a new level, or try and stop me. However, if you chose the latter, I *will* kill you," the Manticore replied. Adam's face contorted with anger and he let out a billowing beam of fire from his hand, straight towards the Manticore. The Manticore flew out of the way easily and slammed Adam with his scorpion tail. Adam flew through the air and landed on the bonnet of one of the crashed cars.

Katie-Anne took out her Radiant Branch and vines erupted from the ground and tangled themselves around the Manticore. The Manticore burnt away the vines with his venomous green fire and lunged at Katie-

Anne. Katie-Anne put her hands forward and a large ball of water formed and launched at the Manticore. It struck and exploded in the Manticore's face. He fell the ground in pain. Katie-Anne then let out vines from the palm of her hand and bound them round the Manticore's front paws. He ripped them off angrily, and swung them around with Katie-Anne still attached and flung her like a shot put into Drakite. Drakite recovered, and let out a blast of purple fire. The Manticore eluded the attack, raised his paw and rocketed towards Drakite. Drakite raised his claws and shot towards the Manticore. The two collided. Drakite brought his tanzanite claws slashing down on the Manticore's red body, leaving massive gashes in his side. The Manticore's paw formed a ball of green fire and he hit a dynamic blow on Drakite's already injured scales. He then brought round its vile tail, just as Drakite brought round his beacon tail. The tails clashed and the two beasts flew apart.

"Give up Tragonzite, you can never beat me!!" The Manticore blared.

"I will do whatever it takes to stop you!" Drakite thundered. They began battling again.

As Katie-Anne went to check that Adam was all right, she had a sudden idea.

"Kashka, we need your help!" she shouted into the sky.

"Good idea," Adam said painfully, as he got up from the car.

"I bet being thrown onto the car was painful," Katie-Anne said sympathetically.

"Just a bit," Adam replied. Then, above them came the titanic form of a huge bird. It was Kashka. He screeched angrily and began helping Drakite. He used his huge talons to claw at the Manticore and pecked him with his huge pointed beak. The Manticore sent a surge of green fire towards Kashka, but Drakite countered it with his purple fire. Drakite then brought his tail swishing through the air. However, the Manticore caught it and threw Drakite as hard as he could right into Kashka. Both fell with an enormous crash onto the floor.

"The bigger they are the harder they fall," the Manticore said, laughing malevolently. "Did you really think you amateurs even stood a chance against me? I have been gaining forces and abilities that would make you're head spin. And now, you'll witness me gain one of the most ultimate forces of all!" He walked back into the centre of Stonehenge. He placed one of the orbs onto one of the columns. Then he placed a second orb onto another column. He carried on until all the orbs were on different columns.

When he placed the final orb onto the column, a brilliant beam of light erupted from the centre of Stonehenge, engulfing the entire structure. The ground beside Stonehenge began to shake violently and cracked. Then, from the deepest crack, a door rose. It was big and completely made of metal and it had a blue symbol of a water drop in the centre. The handle appeared to be made of brass. Katie-Anne thought it was strange. It was just a single door. Surely if it was opened, the opener would just see the landscape on the other side.

The light faded, and the Manticore stood there, looking greedily at the door.

"My hopes, my dreams, my destiny! They all stand before, right behind that door!" The Manticore rushed towards the door and pulled on the handle. As soon as it opened, more light spilled out. It was so bright; everyone had to shield his or her eyes. This light also faded quickly. They all gazed at the invisible room on the other side of the door. They were amazed at what they saw, but none as much as the Manticore. He stared inside hungrily, before entering. Katie-Anne and Adam ran to the door. The room was huge, and was filled by many wondrous objects. Around the walls were golden statues of merpeople and monsters, crystal phials similar to the one Katie-Anne was given stood on tables, filled with various liquids and gases. On a bronze cupboard close by was a mannequin head that supported long flowing white hair as bright as the moon. In the middle of the room was a metallic blue shower, which was precipitating a strange purple fluid. There were also other various objects, like a miniature fountain, which was emitting golden water. A bookshelf on the right held strange objects. On the top shelf were three objects. The first one was a weird charm bracelet except the charms were made out of beautifully shaped ice. The second object was a lily flower made of glass, with a glass fairy sitting on top. The third object seamed to be a figurine made out of a solidified liquid. The second shelf held a variety of books and the other shelves were bare.

Right at the back of the room, supported on the wall was a giant golden trident. It was shiny and smooth, its three forks shaped likes arrows, sharper than the sharpest swords and daggers. A blue velvety ribbon was tied around the centre, and it seemed to flow as though it was caught in a gentle breeze. A single diamond was encrusted in the centre prong.

The Manticore wasn't even paying attention to the other objects in the room; he just kept on walking towards the trident, a mad, longing expression lit across his face.

"This is it! The key to my new power!" he said in an evil whisper.

"Stop, don't go any further!" Katie-Anne warned, a furious expression on her face. The Manticore faced her, loathing etched into his face.

"Nothing can stop me now, nothing!" He picked up a large object and threw it at Katie-Anne and Adam. The ducked out of the way quickly and the object smashed into a shelf, sending objects crashing to the floor. The Manticore averted his attention back to the trident, and nervously extended his paw. He gripped the handle softly, and began to walk out of the room, his face filled with evil joy. Katie-Anne and Adam tried to stop him but he threw them outside back into Stonehenge.

As soon as the Manticore walked back out, the weather changed faster than traffic lights switch from red to green. Clouds formed into clusters, and turned dark and stormy, making it impossible for the sun's light to penetrate. The whole place was getting very dark. There was a rumbling of thunder from the sky and lighting began crashing around the Manticore. The trident began to spark and sent up a bolt of lighting into the sky. The sky gave its loudest thunder, and then an enormous bolt of lighting struck the trident. Both the Manticore and the trident were layered with purple-blue electricity. Then it began to disappear. The Manticore's body was emitting random static sparks. His body began to morph. His back became upright; his arms became almost human, but kept the red fur. His long red mane grew down to his knees and began turning silver. His shoulders and his chest broadened and his body size began growing at a phenomenal rate until he was roughly the size of two small houses. His legs transformed to resemble gorilla legs, except they were covered in red fur. His scorpion sting shrank until only the point remained, and it moved up into the small of his back. Where the tail had been before, a giant orange merman fin grew. All the while, while he was transforming, tiny bolts of lightning stuck the trident.

Finally, after about five minutes it was all over. All that Katie-Anne and her party had fought for had been for naught. They had done their very best to ensure the Manticore never got hold of Poseidon's power, but even their best hadn't been enough.

Suddenly, from behind them, came a flurry of beating wings. All five Sphinx sisters touched down beside them, Solomon riding the Desert Sphinx. The Tao Master was floating along in the air with them. They all looked at the Manticore in a state of shock.

"I'm afraid you're too late," the Manticore spoke, his voice more human, but keeping its malevolence. "I have succeeded in taking Poseidon's power, and there is nothing any of you can do about it!" The Manticore looked straight towards the Tao Master. "And I must thank you for bringing me the wind sovereign. It will save me the tiresome search of hunting him down, when I can take his power right now!"

"You will never do that, we will never let you!" Adam bellowed.

"By the way little humans!" began the Manticore, ignoring Adam's comment. "I forgot that I owe you my thanks." Katie-Anne and Adam exchanged puzzled looks. "When you first started your little quest I was trying to stop you from getting to the keys before I did. Who wrote threatening messages on your walls and on that contraption that transported you from place to place? I did. Who called you in the middle of the night to try and scare you away from the quest? Me! Who sneaked into your hotel room as a cleaner when you were out and stole your laptop? ME! But you did not scare easily. I knew Solomon was on your tail, trying to help you along without you knowing. I then realised I could use this to my advantage. I could use you to get to the keys. Why waste my strength and energy looking for them when I had someone doing it for me. So I stopped the scare tactics and let you get on with getting the keys. I wanted to wait for you to get all of the keys, but when I saw you emerge from the statue of the Sphinx and not bearing the fire key, I knew that I would have to change my plan a bit. So I watched and waited as you travelled from area-to-area getting one key after the other.

When you were under the Pacific Ocean that was when I knew it was time to strike. I wanted to get rid of that pathetic dragon of yours so I could leave you stranded there in the water while I went to claim the power. But he was harder to defeat then I thought. You already emerged before I could finish him. So I quickly decided to see if I could snatch the keys there, but you were too quick and dived. Knowing defeat I fled and waited for you at the Sphinx statue. I fought with my worthless daughter and forced her to give me the key. Then when you lot arrived, I battled you and took the keys from you. So really, it is all thanks to you that I am here today, able to use this remarkable strength." The Manticore laughed wickedly at the long silence that followed his story. The sky was still thundering, the crowd still staring, not knowing what would happen next.

Chapter 14
Battle at Stonehenge

"What's wrong with you all? Lost your tongues?" the Manticore said gleefully.

"So, Manticore," began the Tao Master, coming forward at last, "you think you can overcome the wind sovereign, the five Sphinx, the Sphinxes uncle, two humans, a Tragonzite and a Falcbasilicus single handed, do you?"

"You think I'm single handed?" The Manticore gave a harsh laugh. "Why my stupid little popinjay, I have no intention of taking you on single handed. You haven't made acquaintances with my army yet, have you-?" The Manticore clicked his fingers. The sky thundered again then there was a flash of extremely bright lightening. When everyone opened their eyes after shielding them from the blinding flash, there were creatures dotted simultaneously around the landscape behind the Manticore. The creatures were vile, grotesque, deformed, monstrous and many other evil characteristics. Katie-Anne recognised some of the creatures around, including Chimera's, which appeared to be about a fifth of the population of creatures on the landscape. There were also Yetis standing here-and-there, growling menacingly.

There were also creatures Katie-Anne recognised through studying and pictures she had seen, including Mardas, large vicious praying mantis that were poisonous blue in colour. Katie-Anne also recognised Harpies, large dark blue-skinned women that had fiery red hair that grew to their heels, wings under their arms and talons for feet. They were thought to be a cross between a bird of prey and human women.

The army also consisted of Ursas, large white demon bears that breathed fire so powerful it could turn its victim into an Ursa. Ogres were also a familiar race in the army. Giant green beasts that had lopsided teeth growing below their chins, one large spiralling horn on their heads and their legs were each the size of a small car. They carried large wooden axes that held a bone edge rather than metal.

There were also Banshees, pale-faced wicked women that screeched so loudly it could kill. In the sky, green-eyed black dragons were flying around, roaring and breathing fire. The penultimate beast Katie-Anne recognised was a Lacerta, a big lizard-like warrior with rams' horns. There was one animal she did not know. Finally, she saw a diabolic creature she did not know by sight, but by description. A Senmurv. It was exactly as Drakite described it, part mammal, and part bird. Its savage dog head looking as though it was starving, and would eat as many creatures as it could get hold of. All of the creatures had a band around its leg, claw, arm or wing that showed the Manticore wearing a crown and killing the sovereigns.

"See, I'm never alone! My army is growing bigger and bigger by the day! I even created a monster of my own!" The Manticore pointed to the animals that Katie-Anne did not recognise. They were dark and shadowy and looked devilish. They bore bulging bulbous eyes. "I call them Gloamers. I made them from the shadows."

"You may have your own private army, but so do I! I knew there would be a good chance you succeeded in this mad plan of yours, so I built an army to resist you!" the Tao Master shouted confidently. He pointed his staff into the sky. The Tao orb on top flashed, and all around them there were tiny little 'pops' and more beasts appeared. First there were Fauns, very hairy men with small horns on their heads and the legs of a horse. Satyrs also appeared, palomino men with the legs of goats. Beautiful Cygnuses appeared. They were giant silver swans born from the stars that wore silver helms. Capricorns appeared, however they were not like the Capricorn they saw in the Pacific Ocean. These were land Capricorns, pure white goats with Unicorn horns. Unicorns themselves appeared, looking slender and brave. Three Tragonzites appeared. They looked like Drakite, apart from their markings were slightly different.

An awe-inspiring Chinese dragon appeared. It was deep red in colour, but its long flowing mane, its spines, its spiked tuft on its tail and its claws were all in gold. It was the most beautiful animal Katie-Anne had ever seen, and she was glad it was on their side. Finally there were Nimbies. These were small angels with silver halos and feathery wings. Light, fluffy clouds supported them.

"Adam, that Dragon is amazing," Katie-Anne whispered in his ear.

"His name is Seiryu. He used to be turquoise in colour, but the legend says that when he was battling Tiamat to show that he was powerful, something happened to him and he changed into a more powerful creature. He is the prince of dragons now. If anything happened to Tiamat, Seiryu would become the new fire sovereign," Drakite told, butting into the conversation.

"So you wish to fight me, do you?" the Manticore asked, as all of the good army finished appearing. "Very well, you will know what it is to suffer before long!" The Manticore pointed his trident at the opposing army and his monstrous creatures charged. The Tao Master pointed his staff and his army charged. The two armies clashed and the fighting began. The Manticore smashed Satyrs out of the way and charged for the Tao Master. Drakite was taking on two Chimeras and an Ogre. The other Tragonzites were fighting the black dragons in the sky, fire striking everywhere. Solomon was blasting Lacertas out of the way and threw a Gloamer through the air using his telekinetic powers. Adam rushed off and helped a Nimbie that had been cornered by several Harpies. He clenched his fist, which turned into fire, and he struck one of the Harpies and knocked the others away with a blast of water from his other hand.

Katie-Anne took a few steps when two Yetis jumped in front of her, blocking her path. They roared at her, spit flying from their mouths. Katie-Anne opened out one of her palms and a flurry of small fireballs shot at the Yetis like bullets. The fireballs forced the Yetis back and they stumbled.

Katie-Anne was grinning with her success, when she saw an Ogre trampling by, holding its axe high and knocking creatures aside easily.

Katie-Anne whipped her left arm to her side and a thorn whip appeared in her hand. She whipped it at the Ogre and she caught its axe. She pulled her whip and the axe flew out of the brute's hand. The Ogre looked at Katie-Anne stupidly then advanced towards her. Katie-Anne gripped her Radiant Branch tightly and branches erupted from the ground and tangled themselves around the Ogre, where it couldn't break free.

Meanwhile, Adam was battling a Harpy, when something grabbed him from behind and lifted him off the ground. He turned his head to see with horror that an Ogre had lifted him up. The Ogre raised its axe, just about to strike Adam a deadly blow when it was knocked aside. Adam was released and fell to the floor painfully. Adam looked up to see the Forest Sphinx fending off the Ogre by lashing at it with her majestic paws and flapping her angelic wings threateningly.

"Thanks!" Adam shouted after the Ogre ran away.

"My pleasure," the Sphinx replied. Adam ran towards her and climbed onto her back and they took off to fight a Marda. The Marda slashed at them with its powerful and lethal scythes, but the Sphinx was swift and she managed to avoid being hit. Adam pointed his hand at the Marda and a large ball of Fire formed and launched towards it. The ball of fire struck the Marda underneath one of its scythes and its skin caught fire. The creature thrashed and screeched in pain as it tried to extinguish the fire. The Marda ran away and collided with an Ogre. They both toppled over and with a loud crunch fell to the floor, where the Marda slowly burnt to death.

In the sky, Drakite was having difficulty defeating a couple of Harpies. He took a deep breath and let out a stream of purple fire. The Harpies all dodged the fire and began clawing and howling at Drakite. Drakite swished round and brought his tail soaring through the air faster than an aeroplane, and with force to match this, he walloped the Harpies with it, and they crashed to the ground where they moved no more.

Else where, Solomon was easily blasting monsters out of the way, when an Ogre picked him up. With one swift movement of his hands,

Solomon erupted the Ogre off his back. He then turned around, used his telekinetic powers to pick the Ogre up and threw him into two Ursas that were advancing onto a Unicorn.

Seiryu, the magnificent Chinese dragon was letting out gushes of golden fire at enemies, and tearing at others with his sharp powerful claws. He then opened his mouth wide, and a small ball of energy formed. The sky started to thunder again and rain poured from the sky, which then remarkably turned into snow.

"What's going on!?" Katie-Anne shouted to Drakite as he came down to see if she needed assistance.

"This is Seiryu's special power! He can control the weather!" Drakite shouted over the racket of the battle around them. Seiryu spiralled into the sky and the snow whisked around him. It then solidified into a cocoon of ice. He then dived down like a torpedo right into a large group of enemies. On contact, the ground exploded, monsters smashed everywhere. Banshees, Ursas, Lacertas, Gloamers and Ogres were blasted into the air and no longer showed sign of life when they finally landed. The ice case around Seiyru melted and he flew back up into the air.

"That is one powerful dragon," said Katie-Anne in awe, her eyes wide with shock.

"You don't know the start of it," Drakite grinned. Suddenly a couple of Capricorns landed in front of them, injured. Katie-Anne and Drakite turned around to see the Senmurv advancing towards them. Katie-Anne quickly climbed onto Drakite's back and they took off into the sky. The Senmurv's barbaric dog head growled and barked vilely, and it also flew into the sky. Katie-Anne opened her palm, and a kind of shock wave seemed to emit from her hand. When it reached the Senmurv, it roared in pain and fell down to the ground. Then when the shock wave hit the ground, earth actually erupted upwards because of the force.

"What was that?" Drakite asked in amazement.

"A sonic boom. The first time I've used it, and I must say I quite liked it." But the Senmurv wasn't down for long. It quickly recovered and shot back into the sky and tackled Drakite head on. The force knocked Katie-

Anne right off his back. She screamed as she fell through the air, knowing the inevitable death that would await her once she hit the floor. Just at that moment, something red and serpentine flew directly underneath her and caught her before she hit the ground. Katie-Anne looked around to see whom she was flying on and found that it was Seiryu.

"Seiryu!? Thank you for rescuing me!" she gasped gratefully and relieved.

"Leave the Senmurv to me! Help your human friend, I sense he is in danger," Seiryu replied, in an amazing mystical voice. The dragon dropped her off close to where Adam was fighting an Ursa, and then darted off to battle the Senmurv.

Katie-Anne rushed into he conflict that raged between the Ursa and Adam. She cupped her wrists together and launched a cauliflower cannon. The Ursa twitched in pain and turned to face Katie-Anne. It took a deep breath, just about to use a stream of fire, when Adam pulled out his Planetary Sand, and unleashed the space dust. The sand struck the Ursa in the face, particularly its eyes. It moaned in pain. It raised its paws to its face and tried to scrape away the sand. Katie-Anne and Adam together raised their palms towards the Ursa. Both of them shot out a jet of water. The force of the water lifted the Ursa off its feet and it was pushed along the ground, leaving deep scars in the earth.

The main fight was between the Tao Master and the Manticore. The Manticore pointed his trident at the Tao Master, and a ball of water pulsing with electricity surged from it. The Tao Master pointed his staff, and the Tao orb on top let out the star shaped beam. The two attacks united and caused an explosion.

"You claim to have gained all of Poseidon's powers, yet you only know how to use ten percent of them," said the Tao Master, easily deflecting another attack. The Manticore roared in rage.

"I shall not be beaten by you!" the Manticore thundered in reply, "I'm too close to lose now! When I have beaten you to the full extent of my powers, I will destroy the Tao and claim *your* power as mine as well!"

"Unluckily for you, that will never happen!" The Tao Master charged into another attack and the battling continued enthusiastically.

The armies below were still fighting, neither side showing any sign of weakness. Creatures from both sides lay defeated and in some cases destroyed on the ground. It seemed the battle would never end. The Manticore roared again as the Tao Master blocked another of its attacks. It raised the trident above its head, and from behind him, a tidal wave rose, fifty feet or so. The tidal wave was incredible. Drakite quickly flew down and Katie-Anne climbed onto his back followed by Adam. All the creatures that could fly flew as far above the wave as possible. All the land creatures didn't know what to do. The wave rushed into the Manticore, but it didn't affect it. The wave then struck Stonehenge, smashing the thousands of years old rocks to the ground. The monsters were pulled in and blasted away, killed as it struck them. Solomon was hit with the full force and disappeared from sight. The Tao Master tried to use a defensive shield but it was no good. The wave struck him and he disappeared too. The wave continued going and eventually subsided.

Drakite and his passengers circled above the wreckage, looking down upon the disaster. Stonehenge was no more, only two columns survived the wrath of the wave. Solomon was lying unconscious on top of a Unicorn, and the Tao Master had been crushed by one of the cars from the road. He had been so injured and weakened by the attack; he didn't have the strength to lift the car off him. The Manticore flew down to meet him, and gloatingly stole his staff.

"NO!" Drakite bellowed. He flew down, but the Manticore blasted him away easily. Katie-Anne and Adam flew off his back and landed painfully on the ground, and Drakite smashed into one of the remaining columns of Stonehenge and moved no more.

The Manticore threw the Tao Master's staff high into the air. He pointed his trident at it and launched a burst of energy. On contact, the wood of the staff dissolved instantly, and the orb of the Tao landed on the ground gently. Katie-Anne saw it quickly. The orb flashed then a crack appeared, directly separating the black half from the white. The white half flashed and disappeared. The black half did the same, and the orb was now just an empty shell.

"I've done it!" The Manticore shouted jubilantly. The Manticore laughed malevolently, clicked his fingers and disappeared in a blast of water. His army all disappeared too.

"What's happened?" Katie-Anne asked, slowly getting to her feet. One of the Sphinxes landed next to her.

"The worst possible thing that could have happened. The Manticore has broken the Tao. The balance of good and bad has been destroyed. The world will eventually turn into a place of darkness. And because the Tao Master fused his sovereign powers with the balance, he has also lost his powers."

"Is there nothing we can do now?" Adam asked anxiously, as the weather started to spiral out of control. It started to rain, and then snow, then the wind picked up, then the sun came out then it started to snow again.

"There is, but the chances of it working are so low it is basically impossible," the Sphinx replied, tears spilling down her face. "We need to reunite the two pieces. The good half of the Tao will be finding its way to the dimension of the pure, while the evil half of the Tao will be finding its way to the Land of Shadow.

"Is that what them flashes of light were?" Adam responded. The Sphinx nodded. Katie-Anne was in a state of shock. Not only had they let the Manticore get hold of Poseidon's power, but they had given it a chance to gain the power of the wind sovereign, too.

"Does that mean the Tao Master is no longer the sovereign?" Katie-Anne asked fearfully.

"I'm afraid it does. The Tao Master is now just another average mythical creature."

"What did you mean when you said that the Tao pieces were finding their way to, what was it?" Adam asked, butting in.

"I presume you know what heaven and hell are?" The Sphinx asked. Both Katie-Anne and Adam replied in the positive. The Sphinx sighed.

"Well, the dimension of the pure is sort of like heaven. It's a spiritual place where those who die go if they led a pure life. It is guarded by an ancient city that is protected by a powerful guardian. The Land of Shadow is basically the opposite. Dragons and demonic figures rule it. This is where you end up when you have led an impure life. Tiamat, and her dragon army guard this place. No one really knows how to get there because Tiamat, like the Tao Master, lives in her own dimension, so it would be difficult to find."

"So can't we enter either of these places unless we are dead?" Katie-Anne asked.

"No, that isn't the problem. It is certainly true that you must have a very, very valid argument if you wish to enter such a place. The main dilemma is that you can't enter the dimension of the pure unless you have a good soul, and vice versa for the Land of Shadow. It would be no problem for us to enter the dimension of the pure, but we won't have anyone to go to the land of shadow because no one in our army is impure."

"Won't the Manticore have the same problem as us?"

"He will. But he is very powerful and is a master of prestidigitation. What is worse, he will obviously come across Tiamat in his search for the Tao halves, and steal her sovereign powers, too."

Katie-Anne felt thoroughly depressed. It sounded as though the future was already planned out, and it was definitely not for the better. Drakite got up, and limped towards Solomon to make sure he was all right, and lifted the car off the Tao Master. The weather was still changing as though it was a broken record, and all the animals avoided eye contact with each other.

"I think its time we all went. There is nothing more we can do here," Drakite said calmly, squinting as he walked over to Katie-Anne and Adam.

"Drakite, I think its better I fly them home now, you are in no condition, you're really hurt," the Sphinx suggested, looking sympathetically at his wounds. Drakite nodded in agreement and walked off.

*

Many months had passed since the consequential fight at Stonehenge. The world was a completely different place. Weather patterns caused dire malfunctions around the globe, causing some countries to flood, while others hitting the other end of the scale; drought. Stories of whole towns and cities being wiped out by someone from the Manticore's army were common. The world itself had stopped completely, so eventually everything would wither. If something wasn't done, then half of the planet would die of cold and the half that was facing the sun would die of the heat.

Since the fight, Katie-Anne and Adam hadn't seen anyone from the Tao Master's army. No Drakite, no Solomon, no Sphinxes. There continual absence worried Katie-Anne. The world was facing dark times, and there was a high possibility something could have happened to any of them.

However, not all was bad. Since neither Katie-Anne nor Adam were being called upon to help in the fight, they decided to found their own company. Out of all the press and publicity they received they made a lot of many and bought a skyscraper in London. They now published or created anything to do with mythical animals. They also printed weakly tips on what to do if any mythical animals that were foes confront you. Their singularly best product was the card game they created. Here are the rules.

Chapter 15
The Rules of the Card Game

Both players start by placing one Monster Card in the battle zone, face down. Both players then select up to two monsters to be placed in the Backup Zone. These must be placed face down. The players flip a coin. Whoever calls the outcome correctly starts the game.

*

To win, one player must collect all five key tokens. You can collect a key token for every three of your opponent's monsters you destroy. However, if you destroy your opponent's field monster, and both backup monsters and he has no monsters left to play, yet you still have key tokens to obtain, you win.

To lose, your opponent must collect all five of your key tokens before you collect his. You can also lose if you have no monsters left to play, even though your opponent still has tokens to collect.

To draw, both players must collect the five key tokens at the same time, or both players wipe each other's field monster out at the same time, and neither had any backup monsters.

*

Each Monster Card has six different strengths: Mortal Strength, Immortal Strength, Fire Power, Water Power, Wind Power and Earth Power. A monster may attack with whatever strength he likes.

When a card is destroyed, it must go to its owners Golden Box Zone. Once it is here, it cannot be used for the remainder of the game. However, there may be certain cards which allow you to bring cards back from the Golden Box Zone or require them to be in there in order for another card to be played.

*

The game consists of two card types: Monster Cards and Power-up Cards. All the Monster Card's strengths vary from zero to two thousand. Depending on what their element is, decides how strong their powers are. Here is an example. If you play a card that has a Fire Elemental Attribute, you can expect its Fire Power to be quite high, and its Water Power to be fairly low.

Each Elemental Attribute is weak against another element. So your power may increase or decrease depending on the monster element you are fighting. Here is an example: a Chimera has a Fire Attribute and it is fighting a Hydra, which has a Water Attribute. No matter what type of attack the Chimera uses, that attack will be reduced by half because Fire Attributes are weak against Water Attributes. However, the actual powers themselves do not decide this. An example. If there is a Chimera against another Chimera, they are both Fire Attributes so they attack as normal. If you attack with the Chimera's Water Power, this just attacks like normal because the Chimera is not a Water Attribute. This is a complete list of what happens when fighting a different Attribute:

Fire vs. Fire – Power stays normal
Fire vs. Water – Power is halved
Fire vs. Earth – Power doubles
Fire vs. Wind – Power stays normal

Water vs. Water – Power stays normal
Water vs. Fire – Power doubles
Water vs. Earth – Power stays normal
Water vs. Wind – Power halves

Wind vs. Wind – Power stays normal
Wind vs. Fire – Power stays normal
Wind vs. Water – Power doubles
Wind vs. Earth – Power halves

Earth vs. Earth – Power stays normal
Earth vs. Fire – Power halves
Earth vs. Water – Power stays normal
Earth vs. Wind – Power doubles

This power change only happens to the attacking monster's points. The monster being attacked does not have its points doubled or halved.

The point change only applies for the duration of the attack. When one of the monsters is destroyed, points return to normal until the next monster comes onto the field.

When a monster attacks with one of its powers e.g. Water, you must attack the same power on your opponent's monster. If your monster had a Water Power of 1700 and your opponent's had a monster with a Water Power of 1200, and you choose to attack with your water power, then you would win because your Water Power is higher. Of course, if your monster Attribute is water, and your opponent's monster's attribute is wind, then of course your Water Power will be halved and you would lose.

The final thing about Monster Cards is that they have upgrade levels. Every monster starts at level one, and you must play a level one monster on the field. You cannot just play a level two or higher monster on the field or Backup Zone. However, certain Power-up Cards can upgrade your current monster to its next level (providing you have that level monster in your deck). An example would be you having a level one Chimera on the field. You have a level two Chimera in your deck. By playing a certain Power-up Card, you may take your level two Chimera out of your deck and use it to replace the level one Chimera. The highest level you can reach is level eight.

*

Power-up Cards do many things. Their main aim is to upgrade your strength or level. They can only be used on your turn and on your monsters (unless stated otherwise). However, some of these cards state that you may use them when your opponent is attacking. An example would be the Power-up Card 'Fire Release'. This card upgrades one of your monster's Fire Power by thirty points. A Power-up Card goes to the Golden Box Zone once the monster it is equipped to is destroyed.

You may not equip more than six Power-up Cards. You cannot equip Power-up Cards to a monster waiting in the Backup Zone. When you upgrade a monster to its next level, all Power-up Cards equipped to the monster being upgraded are sent to the Golden Box Zone.

*

There are four very rare, and extremely powerful cards. These are the Sovereign Cards. Some normal rules do not apply to these cards. Only one of each of these is allowed in any deck, while other cards can have a maximum of five each. Their natural strengths may exceed the 2000 limit. No Sovereign Card is weak or strong against another attribute. As a result, they gain no power increase or decrease when fighting certain attributes.

*

There are three types of zone. The first and most important zone is the Battle Zone. This is where you place your active monster. There is the Backup Zone, where you place up to two monsters, which must replace you active monster when it is destroyed. Of course, you can place a monster in the Backup Zone whenever you like, providing there is a free space. Finally there is the Golden Box Zone. A card is sent here when it is destroyed and may not be used again for the rest of the game, unless a Power-up Card brings it back.

*

The game starts by drawing five cards. If you do not have a monster you can use when you start, you must keep shuffling your hand into you deck until you have one. Each turn, you draw one card from the top of you deck. The deck stays face down for the whole of the battle unless you need to search for a card. If this situation does arise, you must shuffle your deck once you have found the required card. A deck can have a maximum of seventy cards.

Only one Power-up Card can be placed per turn.

Chapter 16
The Unbalance of the Tao

In the few months that the Card Game had been out, it made Katie-Anne and Adam very rich. They brought themselves brand new houses with shiny new cars to boot. But still, they heard no news from any of their new friends.

Finally, early one morning, Katie-Anne and Adam held a meeting on the twenty-fourth floor of their skyscraper, when some of the other members of the meeting gasped in shock. Katie-Anne and Adam turned round to face the huge window at the back of the room. Drakite was flapping up and down, looking into the room, indicating to Katie-Anne that he wanted a word.

"This meeting is disbanded! Move, now!" Adam ordered to the room. The people got up quickly and disappeared through the door as quick as they could. Others were still standing in the room, staring transfixed at Drakite.

Katie-Anne and Adam rushed through the door and to the nearest elevator they could find. They cursed openly at the slow speed of the elevator, and forced the doors open once they reached the ground floor. Katie-Anne ran towards the entrance as fast as her high heels would let her. Adam was already outside.

When she eventually managed to get outside, Adam was talking to Drakite enthusiastically. The pedestrians in the streets had mixed reactions. Some ran screaming for their lives, others approached Drakite curiously, and some just stared, like the people in the meeting.

"Drakite!! Where have you been!?" Katie-Anne demanded at once, without even the slightest hint of a hello.

"Well, hello to you too!" he replied with a grunt, a smoke ball hurling out of his nostrils.

"Are you going to tell us where you've been and what you've been doing all this time?" Katie-Anne asked impatiently.

"Give him a chance, Kate," Adam replied reasonably.

"No, she's right. Sorry, I've been busy working for the Tao Master," Drakite spoke.

"Why couldn't we help!?" Katie-Anne asked angrily.

"Because!" Drakite replied.

"Because what!? We're only human? Unable to survive anything the world throws at us! We've been through a lot more than other members of our army and yet we're being kept behind because we're "weak"!" she thundered. Her anger had been bottled up inside her, ever since the Sphinx dropped her off at her house and not told her what she could do next.

"That's not what I've said. In fact, if you gave me a chance, I'd tell you why I'm here!" Drakite replied pompously.

"Anyway! What have you been busy doing?" Adam asked, intervening so that Katie-Anne and Drakite wouldn't end up hurting each other. Drakite grunted.

"I've been doing many things. Trailing the Manticore, finding the whereabouts of the Tao halves, trying to prevent the dark creatures from taking over-"

"Ok we get the idea!" Katie-Anne interrupted. "Why are you here now?"

"Before, the Tao Master didn't want you to help because he didn't want you to get hurt. He did this because there is a very important mission, which we need to do, and he only wants you two to do it. We didn't forget you; we just wanted to keep you safe until then," Drakite replied. Katie-Anne's anger faded, and shame spread across her face.

"Why didn't you tell us, instead of keeping us in the dark?" Katie-Anne asked calmly.

"Everything has been a mess since the battle, so it has been difficult."

"What is the mission anyway?" Adam asked curiously.

"Well, the Unbalance of the Tao has caused more trouble than we first predicted. Ever since the Manticore gained Poseidon's power, his army has swelled. Remember me telling you about sorcerers? Well he certainly has lots of them on his side now, and he has built himself a fortress. A spy from our side told us that he is practicing magic in there in order to help himself track down the Tao halves."

"So what do you want us to do? Stop his army growing? Prevent him from using magic?" Adam asked.

"No, we already have a variety of creatures doing that. You have a much more important task. We've tracked down the Dimension of the Pure. That's where the good half of the Tao is. Remember we told you it is protected by an ancient city? We found out that the city is the Zephyr Kingdom, where the Zephyr Dynasty moved to after they abandoned the Temple of Nimbus. What we need you to do is travel to the Zephyr Kingdom and persuade them to let you into the good dimension. If you can, try and persuade the king and queen to help us fight."

"How can we do that? Surely they won't trust us?" Katie-Anne asked as though she had been given an impossible puzzle to solve.

"Very much like the Temple of Nimbus, Zephyr is in the sky, but much higher up than the temple. Zephyr can only be reached if you cross Falcon Path. It is an extremely long and narrow road. It takes seven days to cross. However, there are also a variety of obstacles along the way you must overcome. It is a dangerous journey, and I only want you to accept this if you are really sure." Katie-Anne and Adam exchanged confident looks. Katie-Anne saw a glimmer of adventure in Adam's eyes, and this was what spurred her to answer.

"Of course we will do it!" she replied bravely, as though she had just announced she was going to fight for her Crown and Country.

"Will you be coming with us?" Adam asked hopefully.

"I'm afraid not. I've already been assigned other tasks. And anyway, I've already told you the Tao Master only wants you two to do it. I will fly you up to Falcon Path, but that's as far as I can go."

"Who are the king and queen of Zephyr anyway?" Katie-Anne asked curiously. If she could find things out about them, then maybe it would be easier to persuade them to help.

"They are King Leo and Queen Shannon. I think, roughly, they are over two million years old," Drakite replied. Katie-Anne and Adam exchanged shocked looks.

"Are they Gods then? I mean wow!" Adam replied.

"But how do we persuade them to help us?" Katie-Anne asked desperately.

"It should be a lot easier then you think. Just mention that the Tao Master has lost the balance of the Tao, and that he personally asked you to go to the kingdom for him and they might let you through to the Land of the Pure." Drakite replied, as though he had answered a wash-away question.

"But why-?"

"Because King Leo is the son of the Tao Master!" Drakite interrupted impatiently. A short silence followed.

"Well, that certainly explains a lot," Adam said quietly.

"I've don't what I was asked to do, and now I have got to go. You will need to sort everything out before we go. I will be back in about a week to pick you up. I'll see you then!" Drakite expanded his wings and took of into the sky, watched admirably by the people on the street.

"I wonder what its like to have a peaceful life?" Adam asked rhetorically, shaking his head.

*

It was quite apparent over the following week how much damage the broken Tao was causing. Every evil animal (which was a lot more then the good) had joined the army of the Manticore. Not only had the Earth stopped moving, but the Moon had too. Then a few days after that, all the other planets stopped moving.

"We are going to have to get to Zephyr as soon as possible," Katie-Anne whispered to herself in her skyscraper, as she watched two flying Capricorns chasing a Harpy outside her window. Adam walked behind her.

"There is just so much to do, in so little time," he said.

*

As promised, Drakite returned a week later. Katie-Anne and Adam left their company in the hands of its vice president. They had both packed luggage to get them through seven days. They climbed onto Drakite's back and were off into the sky. Higher and higher they went. In fact, they actually went so high they almost left the Earth's atmosphere. Luckily, they had their wind powers so that they could breathe in the very thin air.

Eventually, they stopped at an extremely long, narrow white stone path suspended on fluffy white clouds. Stone Falcons stood either side of the entrance of the path.

"There are a few things I need to tell you before you enter," Drakite began. "Once you pass the stone falcon statues, you cannot turn back, the path will not let you; not until you have made it to Zephyr. Secondly, the path stops your bodily functions. This means you don't need to drink, eat, go to the toilet etcetera." Katie-Anne and Adam immediately broke into protest.

"What are we going to do with all this food we're carrying now-?"

"What a waist-!" Drakite chuckled. They agreed to leave their food and water at the entrance of the path.

"Are you ready?" he asked them seriously.

"We sure are!" Adam replied confidently.

"We won't let you down!" Katie-Anne replied bravely. Together, Katie-Anne and Adam walked onto Falcon Path. Drakite bid them farewell and flew off. Katie-Anne didn't know what was waiting for her ahead, but it must be better than what she was leaving behind.

Printed in the United Kingdom
by Lightning Source UK Ltd.
120524UK00003B/412-417